"We don't have to be open about our...collaboration," he said when she said nothing more. His lips curved in a wicked smile. "We can be secret partners."

The low, almost seductive tone of his voice snaked through her like a lightning strike. She felt the thunderous aftermath low in her belly, a shudder of raw, unexpected need.

Agreeing with him would be the worst possible decision she could make. She knew it bone deep. But when she opened her mouth to speak, the word that spilled from her lips was, "Okay."

He gave her another narrow-eyed look, as if he suspected she was joking. "Okay?"

This was her chance to back out, she thought. Laugh and agree that she'd been joking.

But she couldn't, she realised. No matter what kind of fluttery things he did to her insides just by being Cain Dennison, he was right about one thing. He did know more about Renee Lindsey's final days than anyone else in town, save the killer himself. If she was serious about getting to the bottom of Renee's murder, she needed his help.

"Okay," she repeated, more firmly. "You're right. I need your help. And, frankly, you could use mine as well."

"I need you, do I?" His smile made her heart flip-flop.

Crybaby Falls
PAULA GRAVES

MILLS & BOON

First published in Great Britain 2014
by Mills & Boon, an imprint of Harlequin (UK) Limited,
Large Print edition 2014
Eton House, 18-24 Paradise Road,
Richmond, Surrey, TW9 1SR

© 2014 Paula Graves

ISBN: 978-0-263-24462-5

Harlequin (UK) Limited's policy is to use papers that are natural, renewable and recyclable products and made from wood grown in sustainable forests. The logging and manufacturing processes conform to the legal environmental regulations of the country of origin.

Printed and bound in Great Britain
by CPI Antony Rowe, Chippenham, Wiltshire

PAULA GRAVES

Alabama native Paula Graves wrote her first book, a mystery starring herself and her neighborhood friends, at the age of six. A voracious reader, Paula loves books that pair tantalizing mystery with compelling romance. When she's not reading or writing, she works as a creative director for a Birmingham advertising agency and spends time with her family and friends. She is a member of Southern Magic Romance Writers, Heart of Dixie Romance Writers and Romance Writers of America. Paula invites readers to visit her website, www.paulagraves.com

For my mother, who took me to
Noccalula Falls in Gadsden, Alabama,
when I was just a child, engendering
in me a love of roaring waterfalls
and tragic, romantic stories.

Chapter One

The roadside memorial wasn't tattered or faded as so many monuments to the departed were. The simple wooden cross planted in the ground off Black Creek Road gleamed white in the midday sunlight, and the flowers in the resin urn were real, not plastic, still dewy with recent life.

Sara Lindsey crouched beside the small display and touched the big red gerbera daisy in the center of the urn. A chill skittered through her, as if someone had touched the back of her neck with cold fingers, and she nearly knocked herself on her backside turning to look.

Nobody's there, Sara. Get a grip.

Turning back to face the monument, she

silently read the name etched there, darkened with black paint by whoever had planted this latest incarnation in the ground. *Donnie Lindsey. Beloved son and husband.*

Today was the third anniversary of the accident. Some days, Donnie's death seemed like a distant memory, as if life since the accident had slowed to an interminable crawl, each minute stretching to hours or even days. And other times, like now, the raw realization that he was gone forever ached and bled like a brand-new wound.

Joyce must be the unseen caretaker, Sara thought. For her mother-in-law, the wound never stopped bleeding. Her grief was a physical thing, a heavy pall hanging over whatever space she occupied these days. How her husband, Gary, lived with her constant state of mourning, Sara couldn't imagine. As painful as her grief for Donnie had been for the past three years, Sara still managed to find moments of happiness within the sadness.

Joyce never seemed to. Grief had aged her a

decade in the past three years, her pain exacer-bated by the loss of her daughter years before. And as much as she mourned the loss of her children, Joyce craved someone to blame for their deaths.

For Renee's death, there was no closure. Her murder remained unsolved. But for Donnie's death, Joyce had found a target for her silent wrath.

After all, Sara had been behind the wheel of Donnie's truck the night of the accident. And she'd refused to play by her mother-in-law's rules of grieving widowhood, choosing to honor her husband in her own way.

She checked her watch. Almost noon. Joyce, Gary and all of Donnie's childhood friends who still lived near Purgatory would be leaving the cemetery now, heading back to the Lindseys' home for a potluck dinner. This was the second year of what Joyce called "The Remembering," and for the second year in a row, Sara hadn't been able to bring herself to go, even though everyone clearly expected her to make an appearance.

As the widow and part of the reason Donnie was dead, the least she could do was show up and take part in the ritual show of grief, right?

But grief was a private thing for her. She wasn't going to put on a show or stand around and watch others grieve just because people expected it. So she'd come here instead, to the hairpin turn on Black Creek Road, the place where everything had fallen apart, for her own personal memorial. And if she allowed no tears to dampen her cheeks or sobs to escape her throat, there was no one else around to pass judgment on her restrained style of grief.

Bitter much, Lindsey?

With a sigh, she pushed to her feet, grimacing at the lingering pain in her joints, and turned toward the drop-off only a few short yards from the roadside. Donnie hadn't actually died here, at the site of his monument, but nearly forty feet down the gorge that ended where Little Black

Creek snaked its way through the foothills of the Smoky Mountains.

Sara wasn't sure how she'd survived the accident. She remembered none of it, not even why she and Donnie had been in Purgatory that night in the first place. She knew Donnie had been following a new lead about his sister's murder, but thanks to the head injury she'd sustained in the crash, she couldn't even remember what the lead had been or how he'd come by it. She'd spent a month in the hospital, missing Donnie's funeral and wallowing in a toxic combination of grief and pain until she'd finally talked her doctors into letting her go before the hospital killed her.

Recuperation had taken a year, and to this day, though she was pretty much back to normal physically, the memory loss lingered like a big, blank hole in the middle of her upended life. And the memory she most wanted to recover was what had happened in those last few seconds before the truck had left Black Creek Road and spun over the cliff edge.

What had caused the accident? Was it something she could have avoided? The question had haunted her for three years.

"Must've fallen asleep and missed the hairpin turn," had been the accident investigator's best assessment. But she'd never been able to picture the accident happening that way. She was so careful behind the wheel. She never drove sleepy or even distracted by the radio or her cell phone, because her first two years as a Birmingham police officer had been spent in the traffic division. She'd seen a lifetime's worth of the grim results of inattention behind the wheel in those two years.

She wouldn't have been driving impaired. And she couldn't imagine how anything but impairment would have led her over that cliff at such a high rate of speed.

She heard a faint rustle in the woods nearby, and the creeping sensation that had followed her down from the scenic overlook where she'd parked intensified until the hair on the back of her neck prickled to attention. She eased around in a full circle, studying her surroundings with the eye of an investigator.

The woods around her bristled with life, leaves fluttering in the late September breeze that ruffled her hair into disarray. She spotted a squirrel shinning up a tree with quick, darting movements, its black eyes scanning the area for threats much the same way her own gaze was seeking some cause for the unsettled sensation that had set her heart pounding and scattered goose bumps across her limbs.

You're alone, she told herself, firmly turning her gaze back to the road and the long walk uphill to the scenic overlook.

Always alone.

With the skin on the back of her neck still twitching as if brushed by invisible fingers, she took one last look at the roadside memorial before heading up the mountain road.

CAIN SHOULD HAVE known Sara Lindsey wouldn't show up for the graveside memorial. From what he'd heard around Purgatory over the past couple of weeks, she hadn't been back to Ridge County more than a handful of times since the accident.

Thanks to being laid up in ICU, she'd missed the funeral. Even her in-laws couldn't fault her for that. But what had kept her away after that?

A hunch had brought him out here to Black Creek Road and the roadside memorial Joyce Lindsey tended with obsessive attention. And sure enough, here she was, the grieving widow crouched beside the gleaming white cross, her head bent, a glossy curtain of dark hair hiding her face from his curious gaze.

She couldn't remember the accident, people said. Unfortunate for her if it was true, because without any memory of what had happened that night, there was no way for her to refute the whispered rumors about what might have led her to drive their truck off the road and down the steep bluff.

There had been no witnesses. Nobody to say, one way or another, whether she'd been reckless or even careless. The hospital wouldn't release the records of the tests they'd done on her, but he knew they'd have checked her blood-alcohol level and probably even done a tox screen, since she'd been found behind the wheel. If anything had turned up, she'd have been charged.

Her husband, on the other hand, had gone through the windshield. He'd been dead before anyone arrived on the scene.

Cain knew that for a fact. Because he'd been the one to find them.

A few yards away, Sara stood and looked around, her shoulders hunched and her eyes narrowed as if she sensed his presence. He stood very still, knowing that motion, more than the color of his clothing, would betray his location. His drab clothing would blend in well enough with his woodsy surroundings, but a turn of the head or a flick of a hand would give away his position in a heartbeat.

She had become a beautiful woman, a combination of age and tragedy carving away any vestige of baby softness from her features, leaving the fine bone structure in full view. A stirring sensation in his chest caught him by surprise, and he averted his gaze without moving a muscle.

After a moment, she seemed to shake off her nervous tension, turned back to the road and started walking uphill toward the scenic overlook located a quarter mile up the mountain.

He watched until she was out of sight around the next curve. Then he pulled out his cell phone and pressed the speed dial for his office.

Alexander Quinn answered on the second ring. He didn't bother with a salutation. "Did you find her?"

"Yes."

"Any clue why she didn't show for the memorial?"

"Oh, she showed for a memorial. Just not the one at the cemetery." That strange flutter he'd felt in his chest earlier recurred. He tried to ignore it.

"I didn't hire you to be cryptic." Though Quinn's voice barely changed tone, Cain knew his boss was annoyed. In fact, something about this case had been making the old spymaster cranky from the moment Joyce Lindsey had showed up at Quinn's detective agency, The Gates, and hired him to look into the deaths of her two children.

"Sorry." Cain started walking along the narrow shoulder, keeping an eye out for cars coming around the blind curve. "I found her at the roadside memorial her mother-in-law maintains."

"Thought those weren't legal in Tennessee."

"What's legal and what's tolerated can be two different things." Cain paused as he reached the small white cross. "From what I hear, Joyce Lindsey sets up a new one almost as fast as the state can remove the old one."

"She's lost a great deal." Coming from almost anyone else, the comment might have been a statement of sympathy. But Quinn was anything but sentimental, and what Cain heard in his voice was unease.

"You think you were wrong to take her case?"

"Cases," Quinn corrected. "She lost two children. But I don't need to remind you of that, do I?"

Cain tightened his grip on the cell phone. "No, you don't."

"She wants justice. I don't blame her for that."

"But?"

"But she seems very sure she already knows the answers," Quinn answered. "I wonder whether she'll accept a truth that conflicts with what she already believes."

"Just a second." Hearing the sound of a vehicle engine approaching around the curve, Cain edged away from the shoulder of the road, taking care not to get too close to the drop-off. A sturdy thicket of wild hydrangea offered a hiding spot; he crouched behind the thick leaves until the truck passed. He caught a glimpse of Sara Lindsey's fine profile before sunlight bounced off the driver's window with a blinding glare. The flutter in his chest migrated down to his lower belly, and he knew instantly what that feeling was.

Desire. Raw, visceral and entirely unwelcome.

"You think she wants us to confirm her beliefs rather than find the truth," Cain continued after the truck was safely past, dragging his mind out of dangerous territory. "For instance, if we find that her daughter-in-law didn't cause the accident—"

"The police looked into the accident pretty thoroughly. They found nothing to prove the widow was at fault."

"So they say," Cain murmured, remembering the flicker of guilt he'd seen on Sara Lindsey's face as she looked back at the small white cross before heading up to the overlook.

"You think they missed something?"

Cain started up the mountain, where he'd left his own truck parked at the overlook. "Maybe. It would help a whole lot if Sara Lindsey could remember anything about that night."

"How sure are you that she doesn't?"

A three-year-old memory pricked Cain's mind. Sara Lindsey, bloodied and panic-stricken as she lay strapped upside down in the crumpled truck cab. She had looked straight at Cain, but he could tell she wasn't really seeing him. Her breathing had been fast and labored, but she'd managed to find air enough to scream her husband's name in terror, over and over, until she'd gone quiet and still, falling unconscious.

He shut the memory away, not wanting to let it taint his present investigation. "From all accounts, she and her husband had been happily in love since they were both in grade school. Even the people who think she must have caused the accident don't reckon she did it on purpose."

"And the sister's death?"

"We know Renee's death was murder," Cain said grimly. "We just don't know who did it."

"Joyce Lindsey still thinks *you* did it, doesn't she?"

Cain crossed the road to the wider shoulder on the other side while there was no traffic approaching from either direction. "You should have told her you were assigning me to the case. She'll find out sooner or later. Nothing stays secret in a town this small unless you bury it."

"I didn't want to give her the chance to say no."

"She'll just fire you later rather than now."

"We'll deal with that when it happens."

"What's this case to you, Quinn? Why are you misleading a client in order to keep investigating?"

"It's not what the case is to me, Dennison. It's what the case is to *you*."

Cain pressed his mouth to a thin line, torn between irritation and an unexpected flicker of gratitude. "I've lived this long without answers."

"Too long. You almost turned down a job with The Gates because of what happened here in Purgatory eighteen years ago. Nobody should have to live his life under a constant cloud. Believe me."

Cain almost laughed. Quinn's whole life was lived smack-dab in the middle of an impervious cloud of secrecy and lies. Little of what Cain knew about his boss's life and history was reliable. Quinn had spent two decades in the CIA, fabricating an identity as impossible to penetrate as a Smoky Mountain midnight.

He sighed. "Okay, fine. But how am I supposed to investigate Renee Lindsey's murder when half the town still thinks I did it? Who's going to be willing to talk to me?"

"You had an alibi. There was never any evidence to implicate you. You weren't charged with anything."

"Small-town gossip doesn't deal in evidence and legal outcomes." Cain reached the summit of the hill, where a scenic overlook offered parking for a half dozen vehicles and an observation deck with a panoramic view of the Smoky Mountains. "People know what they know, the truth be damned."

As he unlocked the cab of his Ford F-150, he spared a moment to gaze out across the spectacular mountain vista. The sight tugged at something deep inside him, something he'd have sworn died years ago when he'd shaken the dust of Purgatory, Tennessee, off his boots.

Yet, thanks to Alexander Quinn, here he was again, back in the hills he'd left behind, ready to face a past he'd long been determined to forget.

What the hell was he thinking?

"Don't you want to know who killed Renee Lindsey?"

If Cain didn't know better, he might have imagined a touch of sympathy in Quinn's soft question. But Cain *did* know better. If there was any emotion in Quinn's voice, it was carefully planted there for a reason. To disarm him, perhaps. To get him to spill his own secrets.

To prod him into doing whatever it was Quinn wanted for whatever reason he wanted it.

"Of course I do," Cain answered, keeping his tone businesslike and free of the emotion that burned like a furnace in the center of his chest.

Of course he wanted to know who'd killed Renee Lindsey. In his own way, he'd loved her almost as much as her family had. And when he'd found her body at the base of Crybaby Falls, he'd felt so much rage he'd thought he'd combust. She'd been a sweet girl. A good girl, despite her foolish choices. She hadn't deserved to die for her mistakes.

"Keep me informed." Quinn hung up without saying goodbye.

"Goodbye to you, too," Cain muttered, shoving his phone into his pocket and climbing into the truck cab.

As he belted himself in, he stared through the windshield at the cool blue mountains spreading out in front of him as far as the eye could see. Just over the closest rise, he thought, was Crybaby Falls. He could be there in five minutes. Maybe less.

He tried to quell the thought. He'd spent too many hours haunting the falls all those years ago before he'd left Purgatory behind. Too many hours beating his head against an invisible wall of secrets and lies, grieving the loss of his friend and the colossal unfairness of a world where Renee Lindsey had to die while Cain's bastard of a father got to live. He'd buried the boy he'd been deep in the rocky soil of Mulberry Rise when he left Purgatory behind. He hadn't been back to the falls in years.

But when he reached the turnoff to Old Bridge Road, he took a right and headed down the narrow, rutted one-lane that would take him straight to the footbridge over the falls.

A WOODEN BRIDGE crossed Warrior Creek mere yards from the top of Crybaby Falls, close enough to the water's surface that a strong rain could raise the creek high enough to swamp the rough wood slats that made up the floor of the bridge. But even though the afternoon sun had surrendered to clouds and a light shower, the rainfall never made it past a slow, steady drizzle, cooling air shrouding the woods in a misty fog that made the trees and rocks look like an alien landscape, full of mystery and danger.

Or maybe it was this landscape in particular. These rocks, these trees, these thundering falls.

Sara tucked her knees up closer to her chest as a rising breeze blew the rainfall under the rocky outcropping providing her with shelter. She wondered, not for the first time, if she and Donnie had stopped here at Crybaby Falls before heading up the mountain the night of the accident. Had they lingered here, Donnie stewing in a toxic blend of grief and obsession? Had she tried to coax him back to the present, to what he still had rather than what he'd lost so many years ago?

She'd tried to understand his driving need for answers. He and Renee had been close, despite the four-year difference in their ages. When Renee had died at eighteen, Donnie and Sara had been high-school freshman, just starting to transition from their innocent childhood flirtation to the complexity of a high-school romance. At fourteen, Sara hadn't known how to comfort her grief-stunned boyfriend.

At twenty-nine, she still hadn't known how to comfort Donnie. And she'd begun to fear what his intensifying obsession was doing not just to him but to their marriage, as well.

They'd both been Birmingham police officers. But while Donnie had been content in uniform, she'd been pushing her way up the ranks, making detective and settling into a professional life she'd loved, despite the pressures of the job.

Ironic, she supposed, that the strain on their marriage hadn't come from the stress of her work but from her husband's inability to get past that one, tragic moment from his past.

She'd wanted answers, too. But if she'd learned anything in her time as a Birmingham police detective, it was the awful truth that some murders never got solved. Some killers never saw justice.

And she'd had a sinking feeling that Renee Lindsey's murder was going to turn out to be one of those cases that went permanently cold.

"I won't accept that," Donnie had told her as he'd packed his bags for a trip back to Purgatory the morning before the accident that took his life. It was the last moment of her life she could remember before waking up in a Knoxville hospital, drowning in bandages and a relentless tide of pain.

She rubbed her gritty eyes. They'd come here

to Purgatory to follow a new lead. That much she knew.

But what new lead? Had Donnie told her? Or had he kept it to himself, the way he'd begun to hide all aspects of his investigation into his sister's murder from Sara, as if he no longer trusted her to listen to his theories with an open mind?

Had she forced him into such secrecy with her growing impatience? She didn't want to believe she'd made him feel he couldn't trust her with his thoughts, but if she was truthful with herself, she knew it was possible. The more she'd settled into her new life in Birmingham, the more distance had seemed to grow between her and Donnie. His mind, his heart, was still in Tennessee. It was as if the world had stopped turning for him fifteen years earlier, when the Ridge County sheriff had shown up at the Lindsey house to break the wretched news of Renee's death.

She had wanted to understand. But his grief

wasn't hers, no matter how much she'd wanted to bear it for him.

Had they been arguing in the car? Had she let his anger, her growing impatience, distract her at the wrong moment?

Pressing the heel of her palm to her forehead as if she could somehow quell the throbbing ache behind her eyes, she tried to remember something, anything, from that night.

She'd been driving Donnie's Silverado. His baby. He'd bought the truck used when he'd turned eighteen with money he'd made working at a tourist trap in Sevierville. He'd pampered the old truck as if it were a beloved pet and rarely let Sara drive it, not because he didn't think she was a good driver but because he found such simple joy behind the wheel of the tough old Chevy.

So why had she been driving that night? Had he been impaired in some way? Donnie had never been much of a drinker, but he'd had a beer now and then if he was socializing with friends who drank. The police hadn't checked his blood-alcohol level, as far as she knew, since he hadn't been driving.

They'd checked hers in the hospital, of course, and found no alcohol in her system. She'd have been shocked if they had; she had avoided alcohol like the plague ever since one nightmarish teenage binge on prom night her senior year. When she'd vowed "never again," she'd meant it.

The tox screen had come up clean, as well.

But something had caused her to veer off Black Creek Road, a road she'd traveled nearly every day of her life until she was eighteen. A road as familiar to her as her own face in the mirror. She knew every turn, every twist, every incline and straightaway of Black Creek Road, from the old marble quarry north of town to where the road ended ten miles past Bitterwood to the south. She wouldn't have missed the hairpin turn. Not even at midnight in a snowstorm.

But it hadn't been midnight. The crash had

happened a little after nine. And the night had been clear and mild, according to reports.

She hadn't hit an animal. There weren't any signs that she'd swerved or braked to miss an animal, either. There hadn't even been any skid marks to indicate she'd tried to stop their plummet over the cliff.

How the hell could that be? If she hadn't been drunk or incapacitated, why wouldn't she have tried to stop the car from going over the edge?

Somewhere outside her hiding spot came a distinct snap of a twig, loud enough to make her nerves jangle. On instinct, she tugged her knees more tightly to her chest, like a child hiding from detection.

Was this how Renee Lindsey had felt? she wondered suddenly as her pulse sped up and her skin broke out in goose bumps. Had this been the last thing she felt before she'd died?

A man strode into view, moving in quick, powerful strides that exuded barely leashed anger. He was tall and lean, all sinew and muscle.

And dangerous, Sara thought, staring out from her hiding place with her heart in her throat.

This particular man was as dangerous as hell.

Chapter Two

The drizzle had started to pick up, whipping needle pricks of rain into Cain's face as he crossed the wooden bridge over Crybaby Falls. From here, the roar of the cascade drowned out other sounds in the woods, creating a cocoon of white noise that made him feel as if he were the only person left in the world.

He forced his gaze down to the churning maelstrom at the base of the falls, where the power of the water slamming into the rocks below created a perpetual explosion of spray, both constant and ever changing. The official name of the cascade was Warrior Creek Falls, but it had been called Crybaby Falls for as long as anyone could remember and even appeared that way on some local maps.

Legend had it that a young Cherokee maiden in love with a white settler had discovered, soon after her lover's death in battle, that she was carrying his child. She'd hidden her pregnancy from her family until the day she gave birth in the shelter of the rock beneath the falls. But she'd died in childbirth, leaving the tiny infant alone, unprotected against the elements.

The sound of the crying baby had, supposedly, brought the Cherokee tribesmen and their white enemies together for a time, as they joined forces to search for the source of the cries. They found the baby just as he breathed his last. Touched and chastened by the tragic, unnecessary deaths of mother and child, the Cherokees and the white settlers had made peace.

For a time, at least.

According to the stories, if you came to the falls at night when the moon was bright, you could hear the baby's plaintive cries coming from the rocky shelf behind the falls. A nice story. Dreadfully romantic. And almost certainly pure bunk.

The true history of Crybaby Falls was tragic enough without embellishment. Another pregnant girl had fallen in love with the wrong person and died here for her mistake. But there had been no crying baby, no lesson learned. Only death and grief and a gut-churning failure of justice.

Cain reached the other side of the falls and bent to pluck a sunny golden coneflower from a patch of the wildflowers that grew along the bluff overlooking the falls. Coneflowers had been one of Renee Lindsey's favorite. "They're like lookin' into the sun," she'd told him one day as she plucked one and handed it to him. "They make me feel warm and happy."

He pulled one of the golden petals and let the wind pick it up and swirl it into the churning water below.

She loves me, he thought.

He tossed another petal.

She loves me not.

Renee had once told him he was her best friend, and he had thought at the time she was either lying or sadly short on friends. He hadn't been the kind of kid who made friends easily, for a variety of reasons, some his own fault and some not. And his high-school years had been among the worst years of all.

But something about Renee had drawn him to her. He couldn't say they'd shared much in common, except maybe an inborn impatience with phony people. She was from a family with two parents and two perfect kids, a family with a nice house in town and money in the bank. Her father owned a small chain of stores providing automotive parts and service. Her mother had been a stay-at-home mom, always there for her kids after school.

All Cain had waiting at home, back then, was a mean drunk of a father who liked to knock him around and call him names. Hell, he'd named Cain after the Bible's first murderer because he'd been the only survivor of his mother's attempt to give birth to twins—a fact his father had been only too happy to explain when Cain had come home crying after a nightmarish first day of school. "You earned your name fair and square, boy. Live with it."

Taking someone home after school to study or just hang out was so beyond a possibility that Cain had never even wished he could have friends over. And he knew enough about the real world to refuse all of Renee's hints that he could come home with her sometime.

Lindseys and Dennisons didn't live in the same world. Hell, there'd been some whispers and raised eyebrows when the Lindsey boy, Donnie, had married Sara Lynn Dunkirk, whose daddy was a lifelong Ridge County sheriff's deputy and whose mama was one of those Culpeppers from over in Cherokee Cove.

If the people in Renee's circle could barely accept a nice, good-natured girl like Sara Dunkirk because of her family connections, what on earth would they have done with Billy Dennison's long-haired, bad-tempered spawn?

He released the last of the coneflower petals

and looked over the bridge railing. The thickening clouds overhead had darkened the tree-dense forest, plunging the world around him into premature twilight, but he could still make out the tiny golden petals as the whirling waters sucked them under and regurgitated them a few feet downriver.

He turned away from the falls and started back across the wooden bridge, watching his steps on the rain-slick wooden slats. When he looked up again, his whole body jangled with surprise.

Standing at the other end of the bridge was Sara Lindsey, her shoulder-length hair dancing around her face in the damp wind. Her body was rigid, her hands clasped so tightly around the rails of the bridge that her knuckles had turned white.

Cain's heart gave a lurch and settled into a rapid, pounding cadence against his rib cage. Low in his belly, he felt the slow, sweet burn of attraction and wished she was anyone else in the world.

That he was anyone else in the world.

"Did you kill her?" Sara asked, her low voice whipped toward him by the wind.

He stared back at her, wondering if he'd imagined the question. Wondering if he was imagining her, standing here at the scene of the crime like an avenging angel.

"No," he answered.

But he couldn't tell if she believed him.

DESPITE THE PASSAGE of seventeen years since Sara had last seen him, Cain Dennison had changed little. The tall, lean boy with wary gray eyes and a feral sort of masculine beauty had aged into a taller, lean-muscled man in his mid-thirties with the same winter-sky eyes and a touch of the wild. Life had etched a few more lines in his face, but those lines only made him seem more mysterious and compelling than she remembered.

Once a bad boy...

He had always been an object of girlhood fantasies, as sweet a piece of forbidden fruit as Purgatory had to offer. Sara herself had not been immune, even as madly in love with Donnie Lindsey as she'd been.

The flicker of heat building low in her belly suggested she still wasn't immune, all these years later.

"Why are you here?" she asked. He'd left town not long after Renee's murder, coming back now and then only to visit his grandmother, who lived near Miller's Knob on the eastern edge of town. According to her father, who'd kept an eye on Cain Dennison's comings and goings ever since Renee's murder, he hadn't been back in town since the accident three years ago.

"Why are *you?*" he countered, a snap in his voice, as if he couldn't quite control the defensive response.

She wasn't sure how to answer that question. Her official reason for returning to Purgatory had been to attend Joyce's memorial day for Donnie, but she'd known before she ever climbed behind the wheel of her Chevy Silverado that she wasn't going to make it to the cemetery.

So why had she come?

I want answers. The thought formed like a lightning bolt slashing through her brain.

But answers to what questions? She couldn't even remember coming to Purgatory the day of the accident. She knew Donnie's motivation— the new lead she couldn't remember. And was it a coincidence the accident had happened the day before the fifteenth anniversary of Renee's death?

But why had she come with him this time? Her boss at the police department hadn't been much help in answering that question; he'd told her she'd given him no reason for asking for a few days off. The demands of her job meant that most of her closest friends had been fellow cops and their families, but apparently she'd failed to inform any of them what she and Donnie had planned to do in Purgatory, either.

And neither her parents nor Donnie's had known they were in town, though Joyce and

Gary had told her later, in the hospital, that Donnie had called the night before to tell them he'd be in town for the anniversary of Renee's death.

"I don't know," she finally said aloud. "I guess because it was three years ago today. And tomorrow, it'll have been eighteen years since Renee's death."

Cain looked down at the falls thundering beneath the bridge under their feet, his expression grim.

"Sometimes, I can barely remember what she looked like," Sara continued when he didn't speak. "Isn't that strange? She was Donnie's sister, and I saw her all the time, but when I try to remember things about her, it's all fuzzy and distant, like I'm looking at the past through a frosty windshield. I wish I could blame the head injury from the crash, but the truth is, I don't think I really knew her at all. She was just Donnie's sister, the one who didn't want us to bother her or mess with her things."

"I remember her." The words seemed to spill

over his tongue before he could stop them. His gray eyes slanted her way, narrowing as if he'd said something he regretted.

"Do you know who fathered the baby she was carrying?" she asked.

His gaze snapped up to hers again. "No."

She knew it hadn't been Cain's baby. DNA tests had established that much. But short of court-ordering every male who'd ever had contact with Renee to take a DNA test, the question of her baby's paternity had remained as open a question as the identity of her killer.

"She wouldn't say," he added so softly that for a moment, she wasn't sure she'd actually heard him speak. But when he turned to look at her again, he added, "She made it clear she didn't want anyone else to know."

She stepped closer, lifting her face toward him. The rain had almost stopped, but the wind had picked up, blowing damp strands of her dark hair across her face. One strand snagged on her lips, and Cain's gaze dropped to her mouth. For a moment, his eyes darkened, and something crackled between them like electricity.

Then he looked away again, his gaze drawn back to the waterfall.

"Did you love her?" She hadn't realized she was going to ask the question until it tumbled from her lips.

He turned his head slowly, his eyes narrowing as they met her gaze. "I wanted her. I don't reckon that's the same thing, though." His shoulders slumped after a moment and he turned to put his hands on the bridge railing. "I wanted her to be happy. And she wasn't."

No, she wasn't, Sara thought. She might not have a strong memory of Donnie's sister, but what she did recall was that Renee had been full of life and laughter, even when she was being the imperious older sister—except for those last few weeks of her life.

Sara supposed learning she was pregnant must have been terrifying for a girl like Renee, whose parents had put her on a pedestal and made big plans for her life. College, marriage, a career if she wanted it—the Lindseys had been determined to give their children a charmed life, especially their smart, beautiful firstborn.

Renee would have felt the heavy weight of those expectations and dreaded having to tell her parents the truth.

"She wasn't dating anyone as far as her parents and Donnie knew." Sara wondered if Cain Dennison was willing to be any more forthcoming now, all these years later, than he'd been right after Renee's death. Sara couldn't bring Donnie back, but maybe she could finish what he'd started before his death. Maybe she could find out the truth about what had happened to Renee.

She'd been a good detective once, before the accident. And she had a lot of time on her hands now, while she tried to figure out what to do with the rest of her life.

"I knew she was seeing someone," Cain said. "I just never knew who."

Sara couldn't hide her surprise. "You never told the cops that."

He slanted a look at her. "They didn't ask me that."

"And you didn't volunteer the information?"

"The cops thought she was dating me. Secretly, of course." He laughed, though the sound held little in the way of mirth. "Because Renee Lindsey wouldn't dare date a Dennison in the open."

"But the two of you spent a lot of time together."

"We were friends."

"And I'm supposed to believe that was enough for you?"

He shot her a narrow-eyed look. "Did your daddy send you to interrogate me, Detective Lindsey?"

"My daddy doesn't tell me what to do. And, by the way, it's just plain Mrs. Lindsey now."

One dark eyebrow arched over a pale gray eye. "Since when?"

"I turned in my badge last week."

"Your decision?"

The decision had nominally been hers, but she

knew it had been a matter of time before her bosses let her go. She hadn't been able to throw herself into her work the way she'd needed to. Donnie had haunted every inch of the town they'd once called their home, until he was almost all she could think about. Donnie, her questions about his death and her own guilty fear that whatever had happened had been her fault.

"Close enough," she answered.

He cocked his head, his gaze sliding over her slowly, as if to adjust his assessment of her now that he had this new piece of information. "What are you going to do now?"

She shrugged. "I have some savings that didn't get eaten by the medical bills. Donnie had some life insurance. I've got a little time and space to decide."

"And you came back *here* to do your thinkin'?"

She smiled at the first hint of his mountain accent coming into play. He'd been gone from the mountains awhile, just as she had, but highlanders like the two of them could never completely escape their roots.

"My granddaddy died last winter. He left me his cabin. My dad says there's a lot of work to be done on it, and I should probably just sell it. But I don't have to decide right away." She wasn't sure why she was telling Cain even this much about her plans. He might as well be a stranger to her, and what little she did know about him and his past didn't exactly paint him as a trustworthy confidante.

"And you figure it's as good a place to do your thinkin' as any?"

"Something like that."

He nodded slowly. "Looks like we're both back for a while, then."

"So this isn't a short visit for you?" She felt a flicker of unease. Purgatory, Tennessee, was a place with a long memory, and there were a whole lot of people in this town who still believed Cain Dennison had gotten away with murder.

Her father included.

Carl Dunkirk had never been happy about the sheriff's decision not to pursue Cain as a suspect in Renee's murder. He'd seen Renee's pregnancy by another man to be a damned good motive for murder rather than exculpatory evidence.

If Cain planned to stay here long, he might come to regret it.

"I have a job," he said after a moment, not looking at her.

"Doing what?"

He glanced at her. "This and that."

"Are 'this and that' legal?"

His mouth curved, the first hint of a smile since she'd confronted him. The twitch of his lips carved a dimple in his cheek, sending an odd flutter through the center of her chest. "You think I'd tell you if they weren't?"

She tried a different tack. "I heard you joined the Army when you left town."

"You heard that, did you?"

"It's not true?"

"I didn't say that."

"Did you like the service?"

"*Liked* isn't exactly the word I'd use," he said after a pause. "I guess you could say I found satisfaction in serving my country."

"How long were you in?"

He made a show of looking at his watch. "Fifteen years, two months and three days."

Now she was really surprised. The Cain Dennison she knew—through rumors and stories, anyway—couldn't have lasted a week in the Army. "That's a career."

"I thought it would be, yeah."

"What happened?"

He blew out a long breath. "I guess you could say I didn't see eye to eye with the brass, and I knew it was a battle I couldn't win."

Now that sounded more like the Cain Dennison she remembered.

He lifted his face to the wind, narrowing his eyes. "Looks like the rain's about to pick up again."

She knew a dismissal when she heard one. Cain was done with the conversation.

As she started back up the incline to where she'd parked her truck, she thought over what he'd let slip during their brief encounter. He hadn't exactly been forthcoming, but at least he'd given her a place to start looking.

Renee had been seeing someone secretly, and Cain had known about it, even if he didn't know who. Which meant it was possible someone else knew something about Renee's clandestine affair as well, right?

But who?

Buckling herself in behind the steering wheel, she watched the woods, wondering if Cain would follow. Or did he plan to brave the rain that was already pelting her windshield with increasing fury in order to pay his respects to Renee?

When he didn't appear after a few minutes, she cranked the truck. But before she could change gears, her cell phone rang. Glancing at the display, she saw her mother's number.

She could imagine what her mother would

have to say. She'd probably attended the memorial for Donnie, hoping to see Sara there, as well.

Bracing herself, she answered. "Hi, Mom."

Ann Dunkirk's voice held a hint of anxiety when she spoke. "Did you get caught in traffic? You didn't have an accident, did you?"

She closed her eyes, feeling guilty about giving her mother more to worry about. "No. No accident. I just decided to visit the memorial on Black Creek Road instead of going to the cemetery."

"Oh." Ann's pause extended so long that Sara almost began to squirm. "I wish you'd called Joyce Lindsey to let her know."

"I should've." Sara knew her mother was right. She didn't regret missing the memorial, but she shouldn't have been a coward about it. She should have let Joyce know her plans.

She just hadn't been up to dealing with the guilt she felt whenever she talked to Donnie's mother.

"You're still planning to come to dinner tonight? I'm making chicken chili."

Her stomach growled at the thought. "I'll be there."

"Be careful driving in the rain. And don't try to drive while talking on your cell phone."

"Yes, Mom."

As she ended the call and put her phone back in the pocket of her jacket, she saw Cain Dennison exiting the woods about twenty yards away from where she'd come out herself. His head lowered against the now-driving rain, he walked quickly toward a dark blue Ford F-150 parked along the shoulder a quarter mile down the road.

She watched until he'd climbed into the cab of the truck, curiosity keeping her still. There was something about the truck that seemed familiar, she realized. But what? What was tugging at her memory?

He pulled past her as he drove away. If he noticed her parked there off the road, he didn't give any sign. As she started to look away, a flash of red caught her attention. It was a bumper sticker attached to the back of the truck that read, "Never follow the advice on a bumper sticker."

Even as her lips started to curve in a smile, she remembered where she'd seen the truck before—parked at the scenic overlook above the spot where she and Donnie had missed the tight curve and gone down the gorge.

Her smile faded.

So, Cain Dennison had been at the same overlook where she'd parked her car. And now he turned up at Crybaby Falls at the same time she had.

Coincidence?

Not bloody likely.

Chapter Three

"I think her memory loss is genuine." Cain waved off Alexander Quinn's offer of a drink and took a seat in front of the big mahogany desk that occupied most of the back half of Quinn's office. Outside, rain and falling night obscured what would normally be a stunning view of the Smoky Mountains from the window where Quinn now stood, holding a tumbler with two fingers of bourbon in one hand as he gazed out at the gloom.

"Or perhaps she's a talented liar."

"Do you honestly think she'd have risked her own life in that accident in order to kill her husband? I was there at the scene before the paramedics arrived. I know how close she came to dying."

Quinn took a sip of the whiskey and grimaced. "I didn't say she tried to kill him. But she might be covering up what she remembers because she was culpable."

"I think not remembering makes her afraid she's at fault." Cain had spent most of the afternoon going back over his encounters with Sara Lindsey, from his first glimpse of her at the roadside memorial to their wary conversation at Crybaby Falls.

She was grieving, but she didn't like to show it. She was private and self-contained, but in her dark eyes he'd seen the ragged edges of her lingering pain. She missed her husband, grieved for him, but there had also been a hint of frustration in her tone when she'd spoken about his family, about Renee's death.

He knew from his preliminary investigation that Donnie Lindsey had become increasingly intent upon finding out who killed Renee. The passage of years had only intensified his determination, it seemed.

What kind of havoc could his focus on the past have created in his marriage to Sara? She had been a cop, just like Donnie, so she'd have known the odds were against finding the killer after so long. Had she tried to temper his thirst for closure?

Had it created problems between them?

"Is it possible the accident wasn't an accident?" Quinn asked after a few moments. "Whether or not the widow was involved?"

"If the sheriff's department thought it was anything but an accident, they'd have investigated." Cain hadn't been able to make any contacts inside the sheriff's department—a predictable outcome, given his dicey past relationship with Ridge County law enforcement. But everybody in Purgatory knew former Sheriff Will Toomey and Gary Lindsey had been friends since their own days at Purgatory High. If Toomey had even an inkling that the crash that had taken Donnie Lindsey's life was anything but a tragic accident, he'd have continued the investigation instead of accepting the official verdict of accidental death.

"So maybe it's time to set aside your investigation of the widow and start looking into the sister's death instead."

"You know my past with these people. I was a suspect in the murder for a while there, and I know there are folks around here who still aren't convinced I'm innocent."

Quinn shot him a narrow-eyed look. "*Are* you innocent?"

The question surprised him. "Why would you have ever hired me if you didn't already know the answer to that question?"

Quinn's expression didn't change. "Why would you deflect my question?"

"I didn't kill Renee Lindsey." Cain pushed to his feet and started for the door. "And I don't work for people who play mind games with me."

Behind him, Quinn clapped his hands, slowly and deliberately. Heat rose into Cain's neck, making his ears burn with a toxic combination of humiliation and fury.

He turned slowly, battling both emotions, and made himself look at Quinn. "Is that your way of telling me to pack up my things and get out?"

Quinn picked up his glass of whiskey from where he'd set it on the windowsill. He took a long sip before he spoke. "If I had fired you, there would be no question of my intentions."

"You still want me on this case?" Cain tried to keep the desperation out of his voice, not wanting to reveal to Quinn just how badly he still wanted answers about Renee Lindsey's death. But he could tell from Quinn's expression that he hadn't succeeded. His boss at The Gates was a former CIA man with a long and colorful past in some of the world's most dangerous hot spots. Very little got past him.

"You have the capacity to be a good investigator," Quinn said in a tone that oozed reason and calm. "But you have to scrape that boulder-size chip off your shoulder. You tell me you're innocent, and I want to believe you, but you give off an air of guilt."

"I may not be a murderer, but I'm no Boy Scout."

"Your record in the Army was impressive. Your commanders spoke highly of your courage and skill."

"I'm not in the Army anymore."

"So you're only trustworthy in uniform? But once you step foot in Purgatory, you're nothing but trouble again?"

Cain frowned. "You know what I mean."

"And you know what I mean." Quinn finished off the whiskey and set the glass on his desk with a muted thud. "Did you know Seth Hammond spent over a decade as a con artist? Or that Sutton Calhoun used to steal food from the greengrocer over in Bitterwood when he was growing up? Hell, Sinclair Solano joined a terrorist group and spent five years on the FBI's most wanted list."

Quinn was speaking of men he'd hired at The Gates, Cain knew, men who were now vital members of his investigative team. Cain released a long, defeated sigh.

"What have you done to rival any of those things?" Quinn asked pointedly.

"I killed my mama and my twin brother just by bein' born," he answered bitterly. "Nobody in Purgatory's going to give me the time of day. They think they see too much of my daddy in me. And, hell, maybe there's something to that."

"You had no agency in what happened to your mother or your brother at the time of your birth," Quinn said bluntly, "no matter what your bastard of a father might have told you. And *you* have control over whether or not you behave as your father did. You're not a child. Stop thinking like one."

He never should have come back to Purgatory, Cain thought. He'd had a life in Atlanta, working construction. Making decent money doing honest work. Nobody there knew about his past, about his father or his own failings.

He didn't let anyone get too close, of course, but his track record with friendships hadn't exactly been great, anyway. He didn't mind being alone.

He was used to it.

"Think about what I said," Quinn said after a long, tense silence. "If you still want out of the job, I'll see that you get back to Atlanta."

"But don't expect a reference?"

Quinn shrugged. "There are some things even I won't lie about." He turned back to the window, his posture a clear sign of dismissal.

Cain left the office and wandered down the short corridor into the large communal office shared by Quinn's agents. Even after the official closing time, there were still a few agents at work. He spotted Sinclair Solano sitting on the edge of Ava Trent's desk, his dark head bent low as they conversed in quiet tones. Sinclair looked up and nodded a greeting before he turned his attention back to the other agent.

There was something going on with those two, Cain thought, although they made an effort to keep it under wraps at work.

The new hire was still here, too. Nick Darcy.

Guy had a British accent, despite being one-hundred-percent genuine American. At first, Cain had figured he was putting on airs or something, until he learned Darcy had grown up in London because his dad had been the U.S. ambassador to Great Britain. Darcy himself had worked for the State Department, in Diplomatic Security. Cain had no idea, however, why he'd left that job behind to work for The Gates.

Alexander Quinn had put together quite the motley crew. Cain just didn't know where he was supposed to fit.

"Cain Dennison's back in town." Sara watched for her father's reaction to her casual remark. Carl Dunkirk had been a good cop, with a good cop's poker face, but she'd figured out his tells a long time ago.

He leaned back in the kitchen chair across the table from hers. The corner of his left eye twitched, even as he adopted a tone of nonchalant surprise. "Really?"

"But you already knew that."

Her father's lips quirked. "You've gotten too big for your britches, young lady."

She grinned at him, the sensation strangely alien, as if her muscles weren't accustomed to stretching that way. "So, what's his deal?" she asked, giving her own poker face a workout. "Why's he back in town?"

"How'd you know he was back?" Carl asked, ignoring her question. She wasn't the only good investigator in the family.

"Ran into him," she said vaguely.

"Where?"

She supposed it was too late to back out of this conversation now that she'd started it. She glanced toward the stove, where her mother stood stirring her famous homemade chicken chili in a stew pot. "I went to Crybaby Falls," she said in a hushed tone. "He showed up."

Her father's eyebrows joined over the bridge of his nose. "You went there by yourself?"

"I'm a cop, Dad. I was armed, and as far as I could tell, he wasn't."

"You know your father's just going to tell me

what you two are whispering about later," her mother said from the stove.

Sara arched an eyebrow at her father. He shrugged.

"Tomorrow's the eighteenth anniversary of her death. I guess Dennison went there for the same reason I did."

"You went to Crybaby Falls?" Ann Dunkirk turned from the stove and gave her a curious look.

"She ran into Dennison there," her father said, shooting Sara a look that was part apology, part resignation.

"Really? I didn't know he was back in town."

"Y'all don't exactly run in the same circles," Sara said.

"I don't think Dennison ever had a circle," Carl said in a flat tone Sara recognized from her teenage years. Apparently his assessment of Cain Dennison hadn't mellowed a bit in the intervening years. "He was too much like his daddy that way. Anybody with sense steered clear of the boy."

"Renee didn't."

Her father just looked at her. She supposed his opinion of Renee's judgment wasn't something he planned to speak aloud. She'd heard it years ago, anyway, listening to her parents' conversation shortly after the murder.

"I told Gary Lindsey the girl was heading for grief," her father had murmured, not realizing Sara was sitting on the stairs around the corner, feeling queasy and unsettled by the news about Donnie's sister. "The Dennison boy has never been anything but trouble, and he's been sniffing around her for months. Gary should've done something."

"Done what?" Ann had asked, her voice gentle the way it always was when she was trying to talk her husband through what she called "the valley of the shadow"—the gut-burning stress that came from dealing with death and depravity on a constant basis.

"Locked her up until she was thirty," her father had growled with a burst of anger. "Had the boy arrested."

"On what grounds?" Her mother had tried to walk the line between sympathy and rationality when dealing with her father's bleak moods. Most of the time she succeeded.

That time, not so much.

"Stalking. Harassment. Statutory rape."

"She was nearly eighteen, Carl. And nobody knew she was pregnant."

"All I could think was, what if it had been Sara?" Her father had broken down then, the sound of his harsh sobs sending chills up Sara's spine. She'd sneaked back upstairs to her bedroom and curled up under the bedcovers, shaken to the core, as much by her father's reaction to Renee Lindsey's death as by the murder itself.

"You still think he did it, don't you?" she asked her father.

Over her father's shoulder, Ann Dunkirk gave her daughter a warning look. Apparently the Renee Lindsey murder was still a volatile subject in the Dunkirk household, all these years later.

"I don't know," Carl answered after a pause. "He was always the most likely suspect."

"Even though he wasn't the baby's father?"

"That might have been the motive." Carl scraped his empty coffee cup in a small circle across the table in front of him. "Maybe she told him about the baby and he killed her in a jealous rage."

"Did you know he was in the Army?"

Carl shot her a skeptical look. "He tell you that?"

She nodded. "You think it's a lie?"

"Hard to imagine that wild buck making it through boot camp."

"The military can sometimes straighten a person out."

"Sometimes. If he wants to change."

Sara put her hand on her father's cup, stopping him from scraping it across the table again. "He struck me as different from the man I remembered."

"Apparently he's been trying to talk to some

folks at the sheriff's department about Donnie's accident."

Sara tried not to react, but she could see by the narrowing of her father's eyes that she'd failed. Her mother stopped stirring the chili and turned to face them again.

"Why would he be looking into Donnie's accident?" she asked.

"He was first on the scene, remember?" Sara murmured. She didn't actually remember seeing him; she didn't remember anything about the accident, really. But she'd heard what Cain had done to save her life.

And she'd never even told him thanks.

"You're not entirely surprised to hear that Dennison's been asking questions, are you?" Carl asked bluntly. "What do you know?"

She sighed and pushed the coffee cup back toward him. "Before I went to Crybaby Falls, I went to the roadside memorial Joyce maintains for Donnie on Black Creek Road."

"She went there instead of the cemetery," her mother told her father before turning her gentle, dark eyes toward Sara. "I called Joyce after we talked earlier. To let her know where you'd been."

Sara felt a flutter of guilt. "I should have called her myself."

"I tried to explain to Joyce that you deal with your grief in private ways. You always have."

"Joyce wasn't happy, I guess."

"Joyce hasn't been happy in eighteen years," Carl said bluntly. "And she never liked that you and Donnie got married."

It was nothing she didn't know already, of course, but hearing her father say the words out loud stung more than she'd anticipated. "Yeah, well. Back to what happened when I went to the roadside memorial—to get there, you can either park on the shoulder, which is practically nonexistent on Black Creek Road at that point, or you can park at the scenic overlook up the mountain and walk back down to the curve. Which I did. When I got back to the scenic overlook, I noticed a truck with a humorous red bumper sticker as I was leaving. Didn't think anything about it, until I saw Cain Dennison driving away from Crybaby Falls in that same truck."

Her father's forehead crinkled. "So you think he followed you to the roadside memorial, then to Crybaby Falls, too?"

"Hell of a coincidence if he didn't."

"Language, Sara," her mother said automatically, then shot her an apologetic grin.

Sara smiled back, though inside, her guts were twisting a little at the news that Dennison had been asking questions about Donnie's death.

Why would he do that? Asking about Renee's murder, she could get, but why Donnie's death? Was he somehow invested in the answers because he was the one who'd found them after the accident? Maybe he felt a sense of responsibility, as if he owed it to Donnie, somehow, to get the answers nobody had seemed able to provide.

"He's working at that new private eye place that's opened in the old mansion on Magnolia Street," Carl said. "The Gates, I think they call it."

"Odd name," Ann commented.

"I think it's probably a play on the whole 'gates of purgatory' thing," Carl said.

"Someone opened a detective agency in Purgatory?" Sara asked, surprised. "How do they get enough business to keep the doors open in a little place like this?"

"Oh," Ann said suddenly, turning to look at them. "I wonder if that's what Joyce was talking about today at the cemetery."

"What did she say?" Carl asked.

"Well, I was telling her how sorry I was about all she and Gary have gone through, losing both their children, and she said something like, she hadn't been able to prevent what had happened to them, but she'd do anything, pay anything, to get the answers about their deaths." Ann slanted a troubled look at Sara. "I didn't want to argue with her about Donnie's accident, but she has to know that's what it was. An accident."

"Mom, I don't blame her for wanting answers.

I'd like a few myself. Like why we were even in Purgatory that night to begin with."

"You think maybe she's hired The Gates to look into Donnie's accident?" Sara's father looked thoughtful.

"Well, you said the Dennison boy is working at The Gates, and you said he's asking questions about Donnie's accident. Maybe those things are connected."

"Who on earth would hire Cain Dennison as an investigator?" Sara asked. "I mean, even if he was in the Army and all that, he's still got a pretty sketchy background for private-eye work, doesn't he?"

"From what I hear, the fellow running the place has taken on more than one hire with a checkered past. Heard of a fellow named Seth Hammond from over Bitterwood way?"

The name sounded familiar. "Meth mechanic or something like that?"

"No, that was his daddy, Delbert, who blew himself up about twenty years ago. You might have remembered the name from that. Seth, on the other hand, made quite a name for himself as a con artist before he supposedly went on the straight and narrow."

"Hell of a chance to take, hiring a retired con man as a private eye."

"You think *that's* something, apparently he's also just hired Sinclair Solano."

"That hippie boy from California who became a terrorist?" her mother asked, her eyes widening.

"Actually, he spent most of the time he was on the FBI's most wanted list working for the CIA as a double agent," Sara corrected. The story of the radical turned spy had made every major daily newspaper in the country when the truth had come out about a month ago.

"I guess the CIA connection might explain that hire, then," Carl said. "I hear the guy who runs The Gates is a former spook."

Sara glanced at her watch. It was a quarter past six—any chance there was anybody still answering the phone at The Gates?

Her father's sharp-eyed gaze met hers. "What are you thinking?"

She pulled her cell phone from her pocket. "I'm thinking that if Joyce really did hire The Gates to look into Donnie's accident, someone there might want to talk to the only person who made it out of that wreck alive."

Chapter Four

Sinclair Solano and Ava Trent had left separately ten minutes ago, as if they thought they were fooling anyone. Nick Darcy was still here, on the phone at the other end of the communal office. Cain sat at his own desk, trying to come up with a new reason not to go home, if you could call the rented Airstream he'd parked by his grandmother's cabin a home.

His grandmother, Lila Birdsong, had offered to let him stay with her, but she'd taken in enough strays this month. Her current boarders were a couple of Cherokee girls whose alcoholic parents had arranged for the girls to stay with Lila to avoid the state taking them into custody while their folks went through court-mandated rehab. Lila was a distant cousin, according to all parties involved, though Cain had his doubts. Over the years, his generous grandmother had seemed to find more than her share of distant relatives in need.

And not-so-distant ones, he thought with fondness. If it hadn't been for Lila, he doubted he'd have survived to adulthood in his father's custody.

The phone rang. Darcy looked up from his own call, lifting his dark eyebrows at Cain. The number on the display wasn't a local one, and Cain considered letting the answering service pick up, since office hours were, technically, over.

But what the hell—he could use a distraction from his own gloomy thoughts. He picked up the receiver. "The Gates. Dennison speaking."

"So. You really do work there."

His hand clenched around the receiver as he recognized Sara Lindsey's soft voice. "Been doing a little detecting of your own?"

"You were in the woods, watching me at the roadside memorial, weren't you?"

How had she figured that out? "You going to have me arrested for stalking or something?"

"Don't tempt me."

"How'd you get this number?"

"My father. You know him. Used to be a sheriff's department investigator. Tried to send you to jail more than once."

"Yeah, your daddy and I go way back."

"Did Joyce Lindsey hire you to investigate Donnie's accident?" She sounded as if she didn't believe it was true, even as she asked the question.

"I can't comment on agency clients," he answered carefully.

"Which means yes." There was a long pause on the other end of the line, making him wonder if she'd hung up on him. But a moment later, she added, "I can't believe she hired *you,* of all people."

He didn't respond. Anything he said would break a company rule.

"But she didn't, did she?" Sara added, realization coloring her voice. "She hired the agency. She didn't know you'd be the person they'd send out to investigate."

Well, he thought. *That didn't take long.* If only he hadn't gone to Crybaby Falls...

"Does Joyce think I did something to cause the accident?"

The hint of vulnerability in Sara's voice caught him by surprise. What could he tell her? Anything he said at this point would be a breach of confidentiality.

"Oh, right," she said when he didn't respond. "You can't comment on clients."

"Detective Lindsey—"

"Mrs. Lindsey," she reminded him. "Not a cop anymore, remember?"

He closed his eyes. "I don't have any reason to think you did anything to cause the accident. It was a hairpin turn at night. Anything could have happened—maybe you swerved to miss a deer or a raccoon—"

"I've gone over the police reports on the accident. There's nothing to suggest I swerved. It was like I went straight over the edge without stopping."

"Mrs. Lindsey—"

"Oh, for pity's sake, just call me Sara. Mrs. Lindsey is my mother-in-law." Her voice came out in a frustrated growl that made him smile despite the knot of tension in his stomach. "Speaking of Joyce, what are you going to do when it finally gets back to her that you're the agent doing the investigating?"

"That won't be a situation for me to deal with," he answered carefully.

"Have you found out why Donnie and I were in Purgatory the night of the crash?" she asked.

"No. If you saw anyone that day, nobody's saying."

There was a long pause on the other end of the line before she spoke in a quiet tone. "That's a mystery itself, isn't it? Why would we come to town and not see anyone who knows us?"

"What's the last thing you do remember, before the accident?"

Once again, the other end of the line went quiet.

"Sara?" he prodded, wondering if the call had disconnected.

"I'm not at liberty to share the details of my investigation with you," she answered primly, although he thought he heard a hint of payback in her careful tone.

He stifled a smile. "Fair enough."

"If you want to ask me questions, next time just ask me straight out," she added. "Instead of playing games."

"I thought I did just ask you straight out."

"Good night, Mr. Dennison."

"Cain," he corrected, but she'd already disconnected.

With a sigh, he hung up the phone and looked up to find Nick Darcy watching him curiously.

"You're working rather late," Darcy commented. His odd British-tinged accent made the corner of Cain's mouth twitch.

"Yes, rather," he agreed, unable to resist mimicking Darcy's accent.

One of Darcy's eyebrows notched upward, but that was his only reaction to the touch of mockery, and Cain immediately felt like a heel.

"Sorry," Cain said. "I can be an ass."

Darcy's lips curved slightly. "Indeed."

Cain laughed. "You headed home?"

"Thought I'd have a bite to eat first. You?"

"Not sure."

"I wouldn't mind company," Darcy added as he shrugged on his jacket. Unlike most of the other agents at The Gates, who dressed for comfort and mobility, Darcy dressed like a businessman. Or, more aptly, Cain supposed, he dressed like the State Department employee he used to be.

Cain watched through narrowed eyes as Darcy straightened what looked like a very expensive silk tie, wondering how to respond to the invitation. Did he have an ulterior motive for asking Cain to join him? Was he gay and looking for romance?

Darcy seemed to read his mind. "I'm neither gay nor working any sort of agenda. I simply tire of eating alone in public. In a town such as this, a man dining alone provides an opportunity to stare and whisper without compunction."

"It might be your choice of vocabulary," Cain suggested, grabbing his own well-worn leather jacket and nodding toward the exit. "Remind me to teach you a little redneck, Jeeves."

A town the size of Purgatory, Tennessee, offered few sit-down restaurants to choose from even during regular dining hours. After seven, the choices dwindled to two—the steakhouse on Darlington Road near the old marble quarry and a Lebanese restaurant that had opened since the last time Cain had been in town. He was inclined to go for the steak, but of course, Darcy headed straight for the brightly lit storefront of the Lebanese place, where photos of the old country filled the window display, interspersed with wrapped packages of pita bread, jars of spiced almonds and sticky triangles of baklava providing a mouthwatering visual temptation. The restaurant name—Tabbouleh Garden— gleamed in bright teal neon over the door.

"Ever been here?" Darcy asked as they entered.

"No," Cain admitted. "I've eaten plenty of Middle Eastern food in my time, though."

"Right. You were in the Army, I believe?"

"Yes."

"Afghanistan?"

"And Iraq and Kaziristan before that."

Darcy's eyebrows rose at the mention of Kaziristan. "Before or after the embassy siege?"

"After. You?"

Darcy's expression went dark. "During."

Cain grimaced. The embassy siege in Kaziristan had been a nasty, brutal business. "Diplomatic Security?"

Darcy nodded, looking relieved when a pretty, dark-eyed waitress came to seat them and take their drink order. She looked Lebanese, but her accent came out in a pure Tennessee mountain twang. "Here's your menu," she said with a friendly smile. "What'll y'all have to drink?"

Cain ordered sweet tea, while Darcy asked for water with lemon. "I'm afraid my taste for tea is rather English. I can't accustom myself to the Dixie version."

"No worries," Cain said, stifling a grin. "Though you might not want to call it the Dixie version. The word comes out a little sneering in your fancy accent."

"Dreadfully sorry," Darcy said, and Cain could tell by the glitter in his eyes that he was laying on the accent extra thick.

"You're a wicked bloke, aren't you?" Cain murmured.

"I'm told I have my moments," Darcy concurred.

"So why'd you give up all those fancy State Department perks to come down here to hillbilly country?" Cain asked a few moments later, after the waitress brought them their drinks and took their food orders.

"Why did *you* come back?" Darcy countered.

Before he could formulate an answer, Cain heard a woman's voice call his name. For a second, he thought it was Sara, but when the woman spoke again, he realized the tone was

all wrong. Tamping down an unexpected rip-
ple of disappointment, he followed the sound of
the voice until he spotted an attractive, slightly
plump blonde sitting a couple of tables away.
As his gaze met hers, she blushed prettily and
smiled.

He excused himself and crossed to her table,
knowing he should recognize her. She looked
familiar, but it had been a long while since he'd
spent much time in town.

"You probably don't remember me—you were
a few grades ahead. Kelly Partlow. Well, I was
Kelly Denton in high school."

He placed her then. Flute player in the march-
ing band. A freshman to his senior. He'd known
her older brother, Keith, better, since several of
their high school teachers had insisted on al-
phabetical seating. Cain and Keith had often
been seated either side by side or one in front
of the other.

"Right," he said aloud. "Keith Denton's little
sister."

She grinned. "Haven't been called that in, oh,

ten minutes. How're you doing? I didn't realize you were back in town."

He could tell she was lying about that. He had a feeling everybody and his brother probably knew Cain was back in Purgatory by now. Not much got past the gossipmongers in a small town.

"Just been back a couple of weeks," he said, searching his memory for what else he could recall about Keith Denton's sister besides her flute-playing. "So, you got married?"

She smiled. "Thirteen years ago now, can you believe? I married Josh Partlow—you remember him, don't you? He and Keith hung around together all the time back in school."

Cain had a vague memory of a football player with a wicked sense of humor, but he hadn't exactly hung out with the jocks during his years at Purgatory High.

At his glance at the empty seat across from her, she smiled. "He's outside, talking to some client on his cell phone. He says he hates people who talk on phones in restaurants, but his solution is to spend most of the time at a restaurant outside talking on his phone." She rolled her eyes, though he could tell she wasn't really upset. "He's a lawyer now. Can you believe it?"

He hadn't really known Josh Partlow well enough to know whether a career in law was something he should find astonishing. "Good for him. It's really good to see you, Kelly, but I should get back to my friend—"

"Oh, of course." She blushed again, and he got a glimpse of the cute little teenager she'd once been. "Listen, the reason I hollered at you like a crazy woman is to tell you Purgatory High alumni are holding a get-together this weekend at Smokehouse Grill—you know, that steakhouse out near the quarry?"

"Right," he said, trying not to grimace. A high-school alumni get-together? That had to be one of the lower levels of hell.

"Anyway, if you think you'll still be around this weekend, you should come. Saturday, six-thirty to whenever. We've reserved one of the private rooms at the back of the restaurant, and it's always so much fun to catch up with what everyone else is up to."

"Yeah, sounds great," he lied. "I don't know if I'll be able to make it, but if I can—"

"Oh, do try! It would be such a fun surprise, since you've been away from Purgatory for so long!" She seemed sincere enough, but he could tell from the little sparkle in her eyes that she wasn't unaware of what a stir his presence at the reunion might cause. He hadn't exactly left Purgatory High on good terms, especially since he'd made his escape not long after Renee's death, while a whole lot of folks still wondered if he'd been the culprit.

"I'll see," he answered, keeping his tone noncommittal. "Nice to see you again, Kelly." He made his escape back to the table, where he found Darcy watching him with a look of bemusement. "Small towns," he murmured. "Everybody knows everybody."

"She's rather cute."

"She's rather married."

"She's sitting rather alone in a restaurant, making eyes at you."

"Not because she's looking to cheat on her husband, I assure you." Cain was spared having to continue the conversation by the arrival of their orders. He dug into his falafel plate, relieved that Darcy didn't seem inclined to ask any more questions.

Still, he found his thoughts going back to Kelly Partlow's invitation. If he were behaving like the professional investigator he was supposed to be, the invitation to the high-school get-together would offer an unexpected opportunity to dig around a little more into Renee Lindsey's past. He hadn't been her only friend, after all. She'd had girlfriends, too, hadn't she? And, obviously, the secret lover who'd fathered her child.

The mystery man might be there on Saturday. Any investigator worth his salt would go to the get-together and try to figure out who it might be.

But the thought of revisiting his teenage years

was enough to make Cain want to flee town at the earliest opportunity.

"YOU'LL NEVER GUESS who I saw at Tabbouleh Garden!" The voice on the other end of Sara's phone didn't bother to introduce herself, but she knew the voice almost as well as she knew her own. Kelly Partlow was one of the few old friends from her Purgatory days who still stayed in touch, mostly because her husband's legal career had occasionally brought him down to Birmingham on business. Between pregnancies, Kelly often accompanied him, joking that a business trip was as close to a vacation as she was likely to get between her workaholic husband and her three rowdy children.

"What is Tabbouleh Garden?" Sara countered.

"It's a new Lebanese place in town. I thought I told you about that in one of my emails."

She probably had, Sara thought. "Who did you see?"

As soon as she asked the question, she knew the answer. Kelly's excited squeal merely confirmed it. "Cain freakin' Dennison! Can you believe he came back to town? It's all anyone can talk about."

"I'll bet." Sara closed her eyes, leaning her head back against the hard oak headboard of her grandparents' four-poster bed. She'd declined her parents' invitation to stay with them in town, since she'd ostensibly come back to Purgatory in order to figure out what to do with the lovely old mountain cabin her grandfather had left her in his will.

"He was eating dinner with one of those guys who work at The Gates—you know, that detective agency that's opened in the old Buckley Mansion on Magnolia." Kelly released a soft gasp. "Oh, wow, do you think he might work there, too? Cain Dennison, a detective! Oh, my word, now I really hope he shows up!"

"Shows up?" Sara grinned as Kelly's chatter reminded her, once again, just how hard it had always been to keep up with her friend's frenetic mental gymnastics. "Shows up where?"

"Oh, I haven't even told you that! We're having a get-together this weekend. Anybody and everybody who attended Purgatory High. We all hooked up on Facebook a while back and now we do these get-togethers every couple of months. It's a ton of fun!"

For someone like Kelly, maybe, Sara thought. But her friend had always been more of a social butterfly than Sara had. "I'm not sure I'm up for a high-school reunion, Kel."

"Oh, Sara, don't say that! It really is a lot of fun. Not like high school at all. And so many people ask about you, all the time. Couldn't you do it, just for me? This Saturday, six-thirty, at the Smokehouse Grill."

Sara tamped down a shudder as she pictured what a night with her old schoolmates might entail. Still, she hadn't seen Kelly face-to-face in a long time. Since just after she went back to Birmingham after she got out of the hospital, she realized with a start.

She really had hibernated from life for the past three years, hadn't she?

"Just promise you'll think about it," Kelly wheedled.

"I promise I'll think about it," she said.

And she did think about it, an hour later, after she and Kelly got off the phone. Apparently she'd become quite the hermit since Donnie's death, if her parents' not-so-subtle hints at dinner earlier were anything to go by. What could it hurt to drop by, see some of the old gang? If it became too unbearable, she had a car and knew how to drive herself home, right?

She pulled up the calendar on her phone and punched in the time and date before she lost her resolve.

THE EARLIER RAIN had passed through by the time Cain reached his grandmother's place up on Mulberry Rise just below Miller's Knob. Despite the cool night, he wasn't surprised to find Lila Birdsong sitting on the crude wooden front stoop of his Airstream trailer, a colorful crocheted shawl wrapped around her lean, aging body.

His grandmother always seemed to know when he needed someone to talk to, even before he realized it himself.

She scooted over to make room for him on the stoop. "You're later than usual. Long day at the office?" She grinned a little as she said it, her strong white teeth shining in the moon glow filtering through the trees overhead. She knew how odd it was for him to be working in an office setting, even one as atypical as The Gates.

"I went with a colleague to grab dinner. We tried that new Lebanese place in town. I'll take you out there soon. Let you try the baba ghanoush."

"I'll wash your mouth out with soap, young man," she teased.

He grinned back at her, already feeling better. "Where are the girls?" he asked, referring to Mia and Charlotte Burdette, the two girls Lila had recently taken in to care for while their parents were working out their problems in rehab.

"They finished up their homework early, so

I let them have the TV remote. I think they're watchin' some singing show." Lila made a face. "I'm too soft."

"You're just right." He kissed her on the temple, making her chuckle. Pulling away, he added, "At the restaurant, I ran into someone I used to go to school with. Well, mostly I knew her older brother. She was a few years behind me." He nudged his grandmother's shoulder with his own. "And before you ask, she's already married."

"Did I ask?" Lila asked, the picture of innocence.

"You were about to."

"She remembered you?"

"I was pretty notorious there for a while, Gran."

She squeezed his knee. "Was she mean to you?"

He smiled again. "No, actually, she was very kind. Rather charming, really, in a slightly scattered way. She invited me to some get-together she and some other Purgatory High alumni have started holding regularly. This Saturday night at the steak place over near the quarry."

"You goin', then?"

He shook his head. "Not a good idea."

"I think it's a real good idea," Lila disagreed. "You're too much a loner, Cain. It ain't good for your soul."

"Gran—"

"How long you gonna let your daddy call the shots in your life? He's been gone a long spell now. Let him go."

He grimaced. "Believe me, I've made my peace with the man."

"Have you now?" Lila pushed to her feet with remarkable agility, as lithe as she'd been thirty years ago. She turned and caught his chin in her hand. "Go to the party. Look at it like takin' medicine. Try the first dose, see if it helps. If it don't, you can skip the second dose." She dropped a kiss on top of his head and walked silently back to her house.

Cain watched her go, his chest tight with the conflict warring inside him. He knew, gut deep, that the party would probably be a disaster if he showed up. But his grandmother was right. He'd spent way too much time alone recently. It *wasn't* good for his soul.

And, if he wanted to look at the idea more pragmatically, going to the party would be a prime opportunity to pick the brains of a few former classmates about what they remembered of Renee Lindsey's last months and days.

Maybe someone at the party knew something he or she had never told anyone before. Maybe the killer himself would be at the party.

There was only one way to find out for sure.

With a sigh, he pulled out his cell phone and put a note in his calendar. *Saturday, six-thirty, Smokehouse Grill.* He closed the phone and stuck it back in his pocket, gazing up at the bright moon overhead.

Look out, Purgatory High, he thought with a grimace of a smile. *The Monster of Ridge County is back in town.*

Chapter Five

Sara spent the days leading up to the high-school get-together cleaning out her grandfather's old cabin and trying to assess whether she'd be able to get a decent price on the real-estate market. The location was secluded, which could be both a plus and a minus. But the cabin's bones were solid, the need for structural repairs less urgent than Sara had feared, and the charm of the old place had already started working on her, tempting her to stick around Purgatory rather than start looking at bigger cities for employment.

"I still have a little pull in the sheriff's department," her father had reminded her that morning when he'd dropped by to see how the clean-up was going. "If you're serious about looking for work here, that is."

Was she serious? She'd fled Birmingham because the ghost of Donnie was everywhere she looked. How could Purgatory be any better? She'd met Donnie here, fallen in love with him here, married him here. His parents still lived in town. Many of his old friends were still around, guys he'd played baseball with, friends he and Sara had shared in common.

His grave was here. The roadside memorial was here. There'd be no escaping his memory in Purgatory, Tennessee.

But maybe that was a good thing. Maybe she'd been spending too much of her time and energy trying to escape his memory rather than facing the loss and dealing with it.

She thought about Cain Dennison, eighteen years past Renee Lindsey's murder, still visiting the scene of the crime and looking as haunted as if her body had been found that morning.

She didn't want to be that person fifteen years

from now, the one who couldn't let go and move on. She was going to go to the party tonight, renew a few old friendships and enjoy herself for the first time in three years.

The evening temperatures had begun to plunge as fall swallowed up summer in big, gulping bites of cold air rolling into the hills from the north, so she grabbed an ice-blue cardigan on her way out to cover the short-sleeved brown dress she'd selected for the evening out. Flats for her feet, of course, not just because she was tall but because her calf muscles had already had their workout for the day, thanks to all the sweeping and mopping.

She arrived at the Smokehouse Grill a few minutes late. The red-haired restaurant hostess directed her toward a large private room at the back of the restaurant and, with a smile, warned her it was a rowdy crowd tonight.

She tried to slip into the room unnoticed, but she'd been away from Purgatory so long that her reappearance was enough to elicit shouts of greeting, excited hugs and even a kiss from

Logan Miles, one of Donnie's old pals from his varsity baseball team.

"I swear, you don't look like you've aged a day since high school," Logan said with a sheepish grin as his wife gave him a mostly good-humored punch to the arm.

Sara knew better than to believe him, of course, but when she looked around the room at some of her former classmates, now more than a decade older and many married with children, like Kelly and Josh Partlow, she realized that in some ways, a part of her life had been on hold for a long time.

She and Donnie had discussed children, of course, but they were both working for the police force in Birmingham and parenthood had seemed like something they could defer until they were better established in their careers. Then Donnie had started becoming more and more obsessed with his sister's murder the longer it remained unsolved, and the thought of starting a family became such a distant, unrealistic notion that they'd stopped talking about having children at all.

Now he was gone. There'd be no children. No possibility of restarting the clock and moving forward together into the life they should have had.

"Sara!" Kelly Partlow finally wriggled her way through the crowd to reach her side and give her a fierce hug of greeting. "You came!"

"I came," Sara said with a smile and a nod, pushing her bleaker thoughts to the back of her mind. She'd come here to look forward, not back.

Josh Partlow trailed up behind his wife and smiled at Sara. "Hey there, Dunkirk. Lookin' good."

Sara gave him a light punch on the shoulder, wishing he wasn't eyeing her as if he expected her to self-destruct any second. "Back at you, hotshot. Wow, big crowd."

"Well, I might have let it slip that I'd talked to Cain Dennison about the get-together, and he didn't come right out and say no to coming."

Kelly shot Sara a smile that was part sheepish, part naughty.

"You convinced people there's actually a chance he'll show up to a high-school get-together?" Sara arched her eyebrows at her old friend. "Wow, you should sell beachfront property in Kansas or something."

"It could happen," Kelly defended, hooking her hand through Sara's arm and guiding her toward the back of the room where a small buffet of appetizers had been set up by the restaurant. "Oh, by the way, there are a few teachers and other staffers who show up for these things now and then—Mrs. Murphy has been a few times, and Coach Allen and Mrs. Petrelli—so if you have an overdue book from the school library or an uncompleted detention, be warned."

"I'm good," Sara said with a smile, a little overwhelmed by Kelly's chatter but already enjoying herself more than she expected.

"Yeah, you always were the teacher's pet, weren't you?" Kelly made a face. "I don't know how we became friends. I swear, I was your polar opposite in high school!"

"Opposites attract?"

Kelly's attention fixed on something across the room. "So they say."

Sara followed her gaze and spotted a tall, good-looking man in his early forties standing next to a slim, pretty woman with neatly styled blond hair and big blue eyes. "Wow, Coach Allen. Has he even aged?"

Kelly made a face. "And his wife, Becky. We all hate her."

"We hate her?" Sara hadn't known the coach or his wife well, but Becky Allen had always seemed nice enough.

"She hasn't aged, either," Kelly said with an exaggerated sigh. "And she's married to that hunk of a baseball coach we all had crushes on in high school. Lucky b—"

"Sheath those claws, gorgeous." Josh joined them, handing Kelly a glass of wine. "Anything for you, Sara?"

She shook her head. "I'll grab a glass of tea in a minute."

"This is *so* not the place to catch up on everything," Kelly said, sipping her wine, "but we're going to have a sit-down soon, right? You've been gone forever and I want to hear everything about what you're doing now."

"Won't need a sit-down for that," Sara said with a rueful smile. "I've left the Birmingham P.D. and sold my house in Alabama. So, basically, all I'm doing right now is trying to figure out what's next."

Kelly's eyes widened. "Why did you not tell me this?"

Sara shrugged. "Well, I looked for an 'I just quit my job and uprooted my life' card I could stick in the mail to announce it to my friends, but the Hallmark store was fresh out."

"Are you staying with your folks?" Kelly's eyes widened so much that Sara feared she was about to do herself harm. "Do you need a place to stay? Josh and I can totally make room—"

"Kelly, you have three kids, five dogs, six cats and four goats. Where on earth would I stay?"

"Five goats. One of them was a girl and we didn't realize it," Josh interjected. At Sara's quizzical look, he shrugged. "Look, it had long hair and I don't exactly go around examining goat privates as a rule."

Sara laughed. "Well, as much as I appreciate the offer, I'm staying in my grandfather's cabin up on Sandler Ridge while I clean it out and decide what to do with it. He left it to me when he died last year."

"Is it falling apart?"

"No, actually it's in better shape than I thought—"

"Sara?" A masculine voice interrupted her midthought. She turned to find Jim Allen and his wife standing behind her, both giving her the "How're you holding up?" expression she was beginning to grow sick of seeing on the faces of old friends and acquaintances. "Jim Allen. I don't know if you remember me—"

"Of course, I remember." She made herself

smile. "Donnie's favorite coach." Turning to the pretty blonde beside him, she nodded a greeting. "Hi, Mrs. Allen."

"Becky," she said with a laugh. "I'm reaching the age where hearing other grown-ups call me Mrs. Allen is very bad for my ego." She extended a slim, well-manicured hand that made Sara glad she'd taken time to buff the rough edges of her own work-chipped fingernails before coming to the party.

She shook Becky's hand. "Big crowd tonight, huh?"

Jim laughed. "Not a whole hell of a lot else to do in Purgatory, Tennessee, on a Saturday night."

"Good thing the Vols have a bye week," Josh interjected with a grin. "Hi, Coach. Becky."

"Oh, honey, the organizers of these shindigs have some sort of spy in the Tennessee football program if you ask me," Kelly added with a laugh, giving Becky Allen a friendly hug. "They always manage to work these get-togethers around the ball game start times in the fall."

Next to her, Josh gave a sudden start, his gaze directed toward the entrance of the private room. Even as he reached into his pocket and pulled out his wallet, a flutter of gasps filtered through from the front of the room. On the heels of the quiet expressions of surprise, conversation in the room went from a deafening buzz to almost complete silence.

"Well, hell, Kelly," Josh murmured, pulling a twenty from his wallet. "You win."

Following his gaze, Sara saw what had shocked the crowd to silence.

Cain Dennison stood in the doorway, looking like a rabbit in a snare.

OF ALL THE bad ideas he'd ever had, and he'd had some doozies in his day, coming to the Purgatory High School alumni get-together had to be near the top of the list. Everybody in the whole damn room was staring at him as if he was wearing the skins of murder victims instead of his best pair of pants, an honest-to-goodness button-down shirt and a brown leather jacket. His hair needed cutting, he supposed, but he'd combed it neatly enough.

He'd even shaved.

As the stunned silence stretched on well past the point of comfort, he thought about saying, "Wrong room," and heading back out the way he came. But just as he started to open his mouth, a tall, dark-haired woman in a curve-hugging brown dress stepped forward and shot him a quizzical look as she extended her hand in greeting. It took a second to realize the brunette bombshell was Sara Lindsey, all dressed up and looking like pure temptation.

Her shoulder-length bob of hair framed her face in soft, tousled curls, and tonight, some of the color was back in her cheeks. Her dress skimmed her body like a caress, with a skirt that swirled in tantalizing sweeps around her well-toned thighs. Beneath the skirt, the rest of her legs seemed to stretch for miles, ending in a pair of simple flat shoes that should have looked plain. On her, they looked sexy as hell.

Her dark eyes crackled with energy as she dared him to shake her hand.

He took her hand, felt the slightly roughened texture of her palm against his, and felt as if the whole world had dropped from beneath his feet.

"Good thing I'm not a gambling woman," Sara murmured as he reluctantly released her hand, "because I'd have lost money betting against your coming here tonight."

He fell into step with her as she started walking toward the back of the room, careful to look only at her instead of the staring crowd that slowly began to settle into conversation again. The whispers swirling around him invoked his name more often than not, but he decided not to listen. They'd get tired of talking about him eventually, and maybe he could get around to doing what he'd come here tonight to do.

"Kelly Partlow was nice enough to ask me to come. I didn't want to be rude and stand her up."

"Is this part of your investigation?" she asked,

her tone edged with hardness. "You think some-one here might tell you that I secretly hated my husband and wanted him dead?"

"I don't think you hated your husband or wanted him dead."

"Your client does."

He turned to face her. "I don't think she believes you wanted him dead. I think she's looking for someone to blame for an accident that stole her only living child from her."

She held his gaze for a long moment, then her eyelashes dipped to hide her eyes from him. "I don't have anyone to blame but myself. I was driving. Whatever happened was my fault."

"Accidents happen. Sometimes it's nobody's fault." He touched her arm lightly, but it was enough to snap her gaze up to meet his again.

"Then you're here for another reason," she said, her voice low.

"Maybe I'm here to renew a few old acquaintances. Isn't that why you're here?"

Her gaze dipped again.

He bent his head close to hers so she could hear his whisper. "Or are you here to see if anyone knows who killed Renee?"

She looked up at him, her expression fierce. "Maybe I am."

She was tough. He hadn't realized that about her. Really, before now he hadn't thought much about her at all, beyond the basics. Donnie Lindsey's wife, Birmingham police detective—those were just words, really, identifiers that helped him place her in context with his investigation.

The truth was, he had two pictures of her in his mind. One was the Sara Dunkirk he'd run into occasionally at school, passing in the halls or outside waiting for the bus. She'd been a shy, skinny freshman, and he'd been so wrapped up in Renee back then that he hadn't looked twice at other girls. And even if he had, a skinny four-teen-year-old beanpole like Sara wouldn't have been on his radar at all. That had been the sum total of his memory of Sara Dunkirk until three years ago, when he'd run across the accident scene at the bottom of Black Creek Gorge.

His other picture of Sara Lindsey was a bloody, gravely injured woman in a mangled truck cab, screaming her husband's name in fear and pain. And if there was any image of Sara Dunkirk Lindsey that had stuck in his memory since then, it was that heart-shattering moment of fear when he was afraid he was watching her last, desperate moments of life.

The woman standing in front of him fit neither of those images. She wasn't shy. She wasn't broken.

But she was scarred. He could see the faint white lines of her healed wounds, up close. A jagged streak that snaked down the side of her neck. Surgical scars on her left arm where the surgeons had repaired her broken humerus. There would be other scars, hidden by that snug brown dress, constant reminders of what she'd lost.

He knew what those kinds of inescapable

reminders of a painful past could to do a person....

"I can't believe you really came." Kelly Partlow's voice dragged his thoughts back from a morass of self-pity.

He smiled at her. "How could I say no when you asked so nicely?"

Kelly's pretty face dimpled. "You remember my husband, don't you? Josh Partlow?"

"I think we had an English class together," Josh said, extending his hand for a shake.

Josh had also been one of the baseball team members who'd threatened him outside the school shortly after Renee's murder, but if the other man remembered that little detail from their history, he didn't let it show.

A few minutes later, however, when Kelly dragged Sara off to another side of the room to renew some old acquaintances, Josh edged closer to Cain, lowering his voice. "Thanks for not spitting in my face. You'd have been within your rights."

Cain paused in the middle of picking out

something to eat from the appetizer buffet to look at the other man. "I've made it a rule to leave bad stuff in the past if I can."

"It's a good rule," Josh said with a nod. "Renee was a sweet girl and everybody was rocked by what happened to her. When you're young and confused and angry, you do stupid things, you know?"

"You look for someone to blame," Cain murmured, remembering his earlier conversation with Sara.

"Yeah. You look for someone to blame."

And he'd been an easy target, Cain knew, walking around Purgatory like a wounded animal, snapping at everyone, even the handful of people who'd tried to reach out to him.

Josh lowered his voice. "Nobody knew your father was the one leaving those bruises on you, man. Every time you came in all black-and-blue, we just figured you'd gotten yourself into another fight. If we'd known—"

Cain shook his head, not wanting any part

of this conversation. "Doesn't matter. Doesn't change anything."

"Maybe it would have. If we'd known."

Cain pinned him with a hard stare. "I wouldn't have cared for your pity then any more than now."

Josh held up his hands. "Fair enough."

Cain took a quick, deep breath through his nose, pushing away the old bitterness. "I'm sorry. That was uncalled for."

"No, don't apologize. I wouldn't care to be pitied, either. And, just so you know, I don't pity you. Frankly, I'm kind of in awe you got through it."

"It wasn't all him, you know." Part of Cain wanted to leave this place as quickly as he could and find somewhere small and dark where he could lick his old wounds in private. But he'd spent a whole lot of years trying to pull himself out of that self-imposed isolation, and coming here tonight had been a big step in that process. Running away now would be like admitting defeat.

And Cain had long ago decided defeat was not an option.

"You're not blaming yourself for what he did, are you?"

Cain shook his head, shooting Josh a faint smile. "I just meant that sometimes the bruises *were* from one of those fights I was always getting myself into. Don't turn me into a saintly superhero."

"Yeah, no." Josh flashed a wry grin. "Saintly superhero never occurred to me, Dennison. Trust me on that."

Cain returned the grin, deciding he might like Josh Partlow after all.

AFTER SPENDING HALF an hour following Kelly Partlow around the private dining room, Sara had begun to think the car accident had robbed her of more than just her memory of the days before and after the accident. She recognized fewer than half of the people Kelly chatted with, despite Kelly's obvious familiarity with them all.

"Oh, honey, you probably didn't know half these people when you lived here," Kelly said with a laugh when Sara confessed her confusion a few minutes later, after they'd paused in the social gadding about to grab another glass of wine for Kelly and a second iced tea for Sara. "Remember, Josh is a lawyer. He represents half the people in town, including *pro bono* cases. And as the receptionist at his law office, I know them, too. And their families and in-laws and—"

Sara gave an exaggerated shudder. "Enough said."

"And I know some people from these get-togethers," Kelly added. "I've made friends with tons of people who were at Purgatory High before we were there."

Some of whom Renee Lindsey might have known, Sara realized. Maybe the mysterious father of her baby had been someone who'd already graduated rather than someone in her own graduating class.

"Sara, why are you really here?" Kelly asked

softly, looking up at her with sharp blue eyes that reminded Sara why they'd really become best friends all those years ago. Kelly might not be an honor roll student, but she'd been as smart as a whip when it came to understanding people. Sara had always liked that about her. Kelly's combination of insight and forthrightness had kept Sara honest, forced her to examine her own motives.

"I'm here to find out who killed Renee Lindsey," she answered bluntly.

Kelly's eyebrows rose. "You think the killer is *here?*"

Sara glanced around to make sure nobody was listening to their conversation. "I don't know. It's possible, don't you think?"

Kelly took a surreptitious look around the room. Her gaze settled on her husband talking to Cain Dennison for a second, then snapped back to meet Sara's, her blue eyes widening. "Oh, my God, you don't think it's Cain Dennison, do you? I thought he was cleared. Is that why you went and dragged him in here when he looked ready to bolt?"

Sara wasn't sure why, exactly, she'd gone to Cain's rescue earlier. Maybe because she knew how it felt to be the object of staring eyes and whispered innuendos, at least since the accident. "No, just the opposite," she said quietly. "I don't think he killed her, and he doesn't deserve to be treated as if he did."

"Then who?"

"If I knew that, I wouldn't be here trying to find out, would I?"

Kelly sighed. "I hate to think it could be one of us."

It was almost certainly "one of us," Sara thought. But who?

"I don't like it, either," she admitted. "But it's probable, don't you think? People are often murdered by people they know."

Kelly's lips pressed together in dismay, her gaze sliding around the room again. Suddenly, her brow furrowed, and she gave a soft murmur of surprise.

Sara followed her gaze and spotted a tall, lean man in a Ridge County Sheriff's Department uniform standing in the open doorway of the meeting room. His gaze swept over the room, meeting Sara's briefly before it settled on a couple who stood in the corner, talking to Coach Allen and his wife, Becky. The lawman moved through the buzzing crowd with long, determined strides until he reached the couple, a pretty dark-haired woman in her mid-forties and a balding man maybe a year or two older. They turned and looked at him with a combination of surprise and worry.

"Who's the deputy?" Sara whispered to Kelly.

"Not a deputy. It's the new sheriff himself, Max Clanton."

Sara's stomach tightened. A visit from the sheriff himself, looking so grim, couldn't mean anything good.

A moment later, a terrible wail rose from the corner, and the dark-haired woman sank to her knees, her hands over her eyes. Kelly grabbed Sara's arm, her grip tight. Whispers rippled through the crowd, radiating out from the tight cluster in the corner.

"Their daughter Ariel," someone nearby murmured just loudly enough for Sara to hear. "Someone found her dead at the base of Crybaby Falls."

Chapter Six

Sara's father paced the well-worn carpet in the middle of his den, his jaw working with frustration. He stopped suddenly, pinning Sara to her chair with the force of his gaze. "You don't know where Cain Dennison was before seven o'clock last night, do you?"

"He's not a likely suspect, Dad."

"You don't know that. He's been back in town almost two weeks now. God only knows what he's been up to all that time."

"You want me to find out?"

Carl frowned at her. "You're not a cop anymore."

"Neither are you," she pointed out reasonably, but her answer only deepened his frown.

"Maybe I would be if that new sheriff hadn't come to town."

"He didn't force you out, did he?"

Carl sighed, sinking into the armchair across from her. "No. I just saw the writing on the wall. Everything's technology-based these days. Legwork and good old-fashioned instinct aren't valuable commodities anymore."

"And your instincts are telling you that Cain Dennison killed an eighteen-year-old girl he didn't even know?"

"You don't know he didn't know her."

"And you don't know he did." Sara leaned forward, putting her hand on her father's arm. "If she hadn't been found at the base of Crybaby Falls, would it even have occurred to you to suspect Dennison?"

"No. But she was. And that's too damned close to what happened to Renee Lindsey."

"I know." She sat back, her own stomach in

a tight knot. She'd gone to the get-together the night before hoping to find a new suspect in Renee's murder. But now, she was beginning to wonder if what she'd found, instead, was a brand-new wrinkle to the old mystery.

Could the two murders, eighteen years apart, be connected? The most recent murder victim, Ariel Burke, had been an infant when Renee Lindsey had died. Was it really possible the same person had killed both women? Or had someone copied Purgatory's most infamous unsolved murder to throw the cops off the trail?

"I wish I could tag along for the investigation," she murmured. She saw a similar longing shining in her father's dark eyes.

"You could always apply for a job at the sheriff's department," Carl pointed out.

"Don't give her any ideas." Sara's mother stood in the doorway of the den, her hands on her hips. "Carl, Brad Ellis is here."

Sara glanced at her father. "Brad Ellis from the cop shop?"

"Send him on back," Carl said.

Ann gave her husband a troubled look before she left.

"Is he still with the sheriff's department?" Sara asked.

"Sure am, Scooter," a familiar voice boomed from behind her.

Sara turned to see her father's old partner standing in the doorway, a grin carving lines into his rugged face. Returning the grin, she jumped up to give him a hug. "I swear, if you weren't already married to the prettiest woman in Ridge County, I'd have a go at you myself."

"And if I weren't married to the best shot in Ridge County, I might take you up on it." He gave her a quick kiss on the cheek, then looked at Carl. His grin faded. "Sarge."

"I take it this isn't a friendly visit?"

Leaving his arm draped over Sara's shoulders, Brad shook his head. "'Fraid not. I need to pick your brain about an old case."

"The Renee Lindsey murder?" Sara asked.

Brad gave her a sharp look. "I really shouldn't say—"

"She was a cop for years. In fact, your new sheriff would be a fool not to snatch her up and make her your new lead investigator." Her father's voice was edged with pride that made Sara's chest swell a little. "Whatever you want to say to me, you can say to her."

Brad gave her a long, considering look, a hint of apology in his eyes when he finally said, "I reckon I'm still thinking of you as that kid with braces and skinned-up knees who used to tag along after your daddy everywhere he went."

"Lost the braces years ago. Wish I could say the same about the skinned-up knees." She waved him toward the chair she'd occupied when he arrived, taking the wide ottoman next to her father's chair.

Brad settled his muscular bulk into the chair and leaned forward as Carl sat across from him.

"Y'all know a hiker found Ariel Burke's body at the base of Crybaby Falls last night, I reckon."

Carl and Sara nodded in unison.

"The medical examiner conducted the autopsy this morning. Cause of death was ligature strangulation."

Same C.O.D. as Renee Lindsey, Sara thought. "Is that why you need Dad's help? Because it's so similar to what happened to Renee Lindsey, and Dad was the principal investigator on that case?"

Brad passed one large hand across his mouth, as if he was reluctant to answer. Sara's gut tightened as she realized there was something else, something that made Brad look damned near haunted.

"Ariel Burke was two months pregnant."

Carl spat out a profanity Sara had never heard him use before.

"You're doing a DNA test to determine paternity?" she asked.

Brad nodded. "She broke up with her boyfriend about two months ago, so we're looking real hard at him, of course, but—"

"Has anyone talked to Cain Dennison?" Carl interrupted.

Sara looked at her father. "Dad—"

"First person we questioned," Brad answered. "He alibied out."

"Alibis can be faked."

"He's not the killer, Carl." Brad's voice took on a soothing tone that Sara knew would probably infuriate her father. "Ariel Burke's parents saw her yesterday morning at eleven when she left to go to cheerleader practice at the high school. She was there until just after one. So we know she couldn't have been killed before then. But from one to five yesterday, Dennison was at a training seminar at The Gates. Ten different agents there can account for his whereabouts, and there's video evidence, as well. The M.E. says Ariel Burke's time of death was around four yesterday afternoon. There's no way Dennison was involved."

"It doesn't mean he didn't kill Renee Lindsey."

"It doesn't," Brad agreed. "But right now, we have to look at the possibility that the same person who killed Renee also killed Ariel. The similarities between the murders—"

"Could be a coincidence," Carl finished for him.

"Could be. That's why I'm here. You know more about the Renee Lindsey murder than anyone else. The sheriff wants you to consult on the investigation."

Carl looked at Sara, his expression hard to read. When he spoke, she could hear the conflict in his tone. "I promised Ann when I retired that I'd stay retired."

"You won't be policing. You'll be consulting."

"You don't know what that case did to me."

"I remember," Brad said quietly. "I might not have been on the force when it happened, but I worked with you for nearly fifteen years. I know it haunted you. It haunted the whole sheriff's department."

Sara closed her eyes, remembering the way her father had obsessed over that one unsolved murder, as if he took her death as a personal affront.

Maybe he had, in a way. He'd liked Donnie, treated him like a son. He'd seen the way the murder had shattered Donnie's family, transformed his parents from confident, socially active people to haunted recluses whose only social interactions revolved around memorializing their murdered daughter.

"Okay. I'll consult. But not for a fee."

"The sheriff will insist."

"Tell him to put my fee in the sheriff's benevolence fund."

Brad nodded. "He wants you at the station this afternoon at three. You'll be there?"

"I'll be there."

Brad rose and shook Carl's hand. Sara walked him to the door, her father trailing behind.

Ann eyed them warily as they passed through the kitchen on their way to the front door. For the first time since she'd come back to Purgatory, Sara wondered just how much pressure her father's job had put on his marriage while she wasn't paying attention.

"Rita told me to remind you about next Saturday," Brad said to Sara's mother, who was looking at Sara's father with troubled eyes.

Ann turned her gaze to Brad. "Right. Tell her I'll be there by four." She managed a weak smile.

Brad turned to Sara and gave her a quick kiss on her forehead. "Good to see you back in town, Scooter. Think you'll stick around?"

"We'll see," Sara answered with a smile.

After Brad had gone, she turned to look at her parents. They were staring at each other across the kitchen, tension brewing between them like a mountain storm.

"I can be your go-between," Sara said. "You don't even have to step foot in the cop shop."

Both of her parents turned to look at her. "You were all wrapped up in Donnie and his reaction. You don't remember what it was like for your father," Ann said.

"You're right. I don't." Sara put her hand on

her father's shoulder, surprised to feel a tremble in his muscles. She looked up at him, saw the haunted look in his eyes, and felt an answering shiver run through her. "Dad, if this is going to be a problem—"

"I let her down." Carl looked at her, his eyes dark with regret. "I let you down. And Donnie. Don't you think I know what brought y'all here the night of the accident? He was still looking for his sister's killer."

"I thought you didn't know why we were here."

"I didn't know what you were doing while you were here. But you weren't here to see us. And Donnie's parents said you didn't come to see them, either. So there was only one possible reason left."

"Did that poor girl's murder have something to do with Renee's murder?" Ann asked. "Is that why Brad was here?"

"We don't know," Sara answered honestly.

The look her mother shot her way sent a flutter of guilt rippling through her chest. "You're getting sucked into this, too, aren't you?"

"We need answers," Carl said quietly.

"Can't someone else get the answers? Why does it have to be the two of you?"

Sara looked at her father, feeling helpless. She knew her mother's concern was fueled by the same kind of love that had driven Donnie to seek his sister's killer with relentless abandon.

"If I'd been killed when I was eighteen," she said softly, "would you be able to put my unsolved murder behind you and move on with your life?"

Her mother blanched as if Sara had struck her. "God, Sara."

"That's what Donnie was dealing with. I may not know what it was like with Dad and the case, but I know what it was like for Donnie all those years." She crossed to her mother and took her hands. "I don't remember the night of the accident, and until I get some answers about it, I'm going to keep thinking it was my fault somehow. I know he came here because of

Renee's murder. But the details are hidden from me, and I can't live with that."

Ann closed her eyes, emotional pain lining her pretty face. "I don't want to lose either of you."

Sara hugged her. "Dad and I will watch each other's backs. I promise."

Ann's arms tightened around Sara's waist, pulling her closer. "I'm glad you're back in town, for however long you stay. I've missed you more than you know."

Guilt crept back, a reminder of how much she'd closed herself off from everyone she loved over the past three years. She'd come back to Purgatory because she didn't have anywhere else to go, but the longer she stayed, the more she realized just how much she'd missed her little hometown while she was gone.

"I think I'm pretty glad to be back, too," she admitted, giving her mother a quick kiss on the cheek. Letting go, she turned to her father. "Let me be your liaison with the sheriff's department, Dad. It'll give me a good excuse to get in on the investigation, and it'll make Mom happy. Win-win."

Her father managed a grudging smile. "Got it all figured out, have you?"

"She's your daughter," Ann said.

By the time they sat down at the kitchen table for a lunch of soup and sandwiches, the earlier tension had mostly disappeared, and the conversation wandered away from murder to talk of high-school football—Purgatory High was supposed to be a contender for a state championship in their division—and the upcoming Mountain Moms charity hoedown. "Rita roped me into helping with the setup down at the civic center," Ann told Sara with a rueful smile. "I knew I shouldn't have retired early. Apparently it makes me the go-to gal for anything around town that requires a volunteer."

"Don't let her fool you—she's about as excited about that hoedown as Rita is." Carl shot his wife an affectionate smile. "She's everybody's hero, too, because she talked the Meades from up in Kentucky to come down to play for the dancing."

Sara raised her eyebrows at her mother. "Wow, the Meades, huh? I thought they never left that little place of theirs in Cumberland." When she and her brother, Patrick, were younger, her parents had taken them up to the Meade Motor Inn in Cumberland, Kentucky, several times to take in the live bluegrass music. "Remember how Patrick decided he wanted to be a banjo player and join the Meades?"

Her father grimaced. "That banjo cost us a fortune and he never picked it up again after the first try."

"I never made it as a singer, either," Sara said with mock regret. "So how'd you score the coup, Mom?"

"Last time your dad and I were up there, I got to talking to Nola Meade. Seems her kids are wanting to go mainstream with their music once they're old enough to leave the nest, so Nola and Del figured it might be good for their future careers if the family got out of Kentucky now and then to give the kids some exposure. So when Rita tasked me with finding a band for the hoedown, I gave Nola a call."

"Yeah, little Purgatory, Tennessee's going to give those kids a lot of exposure," Sara said with an arch of her eyebrow.

Ann smiled placidly. "Well, see, Beeson Lombard of MuCity Records happens to be a Purgatory native. We went to high school together. So when I called up my old high-school friend—"

"Boyfriend," her father elaborated with a grumble.

"—and told him I was helping organize a Smoky Mountain charity fund-raiser and could get him a hot new country act to listen to if he'd like to show up for the event," Ann continued with a smile, "how could he say no?"

"Oh, you're good at this," Sara said with a grin. "No wonder you get roped into organizing things."

"You're still going to be around this weekend, aren't you?" Ann asked. "You should come. You love the Meades."

"I'll come," Sara said, though it was her desire to please her mother more than her love for the Meades and their bluegrass that made the decision for her. After the stress of the Purgatory High School get-together, and the tragic finale of that particular social outing, Sara wasn't in a hurry to crawl out of her hermit hole again anytime soon.

By the time she headed back to her grandfather's cabin to resume her cleaning, her parents were mostly back to their smiling, affectionate selves, lightening her mood as she navigated the twisting road up to her inherited cabin. She almost felt like her old self for the first time since the accident.

She should have known it couldn't last.

As she topped the last rise and the cabin came into view, she saw a dark blue Ford F-150 truck parked in the gravel drive. Its driver sat on the steps of the cabin's sprawling front porch, his elbows resting on his knees as he watched her park her truck and slide from the cab.

"You lost?" she asked as she slowly approached the porch steps.

Cain looked up at her, eyes squinting against the afternoon sun slanting through the evergreens that cocooned the cabin. "No. I asked for directions."

She stopped in front of him, pocketing her truck keys. "From whom?"

"Your friend Kelly. Apparently she has a matchmaking streak." He gave her a mock stern look. "Not very discriminating in her choice of suitors for you, though. You should talk to her about that."

His tone was light enough, but a darker emotion roiled beneath his words. He hadn't come here for a reason as frivolous as courtship.

"What do you want?"

"The Ridge County Medical Examiner's office is as leaky as an old rowboat," he said, rising to let her go up the steps. He followed her to the door, his footsteps making the old boards creak. "The girl was strangled. And she was pregnant."

She stopped at the locked front door and turned to look at him. "The M.E.'s office isn't *that* leaky."

"My boss knows people."

Right, she thought. *The Gates.* When she had a chance to concentrate on something besides solving Renee Lindsey's murder, she should take a harder look at the new P.I. agency in town. She had a feeling it wasn't quite as ordinary an operation as the people in town seemed to think.

"I can neither confirm nor deny any of that." She turned her back on him as she unlocked the dead bolt, hoping he'd take her words and posture for the dismissal she intended.

He didn't. His hand covered hers as she reached for the doorknob. "Know what I'm wondering?"

She turned to look at him, her heart thudding heavily in her chest. "What are you wondering?"

"I'm wondering whether, once the M.E.'s office gets the DNA results on Ariel Burke's unborn child, they discover Ariel's baby and Renee's baby had the same daddy."

Chapter Seven

Cain could see in Sara's expression that the same thought had already occurred to her. How could it not? Two teenage girls, both pregnant, murdered by strangulation at Crybaby Falls? Sure, there were eighteen years between the murders, but Purgatory wasn't like a big city where murders happened every day.

"Don't jump to conclusions," Sara warned, as if reading his mind. She opened the door and gave a brief, forward nod of her head. He took that as an invitation and followed her into the cabin.

He wasn't sure what he'd expected from the old place, given the time-worn state of its weathered exterior, but inside, the cabin offered a rustic, welcoming warmth. Colorful woven rugs hung like art softened the exposed log walls. The sofa was old, with a patina of use, but when Sara waved him to it, the springs were still good and the cushions just the right balance between soft and firm.

"The last thing you need to do is stick your nose into this case," Sara said without preamble.

"It's what I'm paid to do."

"A lot of cops never stopped thinking you got away with murder eighteen years ago," Sara reminded him as she settled in an overstuffed armchair across from the sofa. She tucked her legs up under her, displaying a distracting level of limberness that drew his gaze to the toned curve of her thighs so temptingly displayed by her snug jeans.

He dragged his gaze back up to meet hers. "Your father, you mean."

"He wasn't the only one."

"Too bad, because I had nothing to do with Renee's murder."

"Your alibi was shaky."

What was this, an interrogation? Did she think he was guilty of killing Renee, too? "What did you do, talk your daddy into letting you look at his files on the case?"

"As a matter of fact, yes. I spent the morning reading his notes on the case." Her lips tightened into a thin line of annoyance at his tone.

Good, he thought. *Don't want to be pissed off all by my lonesome.* "I'd have thought you of all people would have the details memorized, since she was family."

"I was fourteen when she died. My dad didn't exactly bring his work home to us. He wanted to keep us separate from that world."

"But you went and became a cop, anyway."

"Yeah." She plucked at the hem of her T-shirt, the movement stretching the cotton fabric over her firm, round breasts. He averted his gaze from the tempting sight, waiting for her to continue.

He heard her soft sigh. "Before this morning, most of what I knew about the case came from

Donnie. But he wasn't capable of being objective about his sister's murder."

"Did he think I was the killer?"

She looked surprised by the question. "No. He thought his parents were grasping at straws trying to get the police to keep after you. Renee had only good things to say about you. She told him people didn't know who you really were, how nice you could be."

Tears pricked his eyes, catching him off guard. He looked down at his hands and cleared his throat. "I was home with my father the day she died."

"You didn't mention your father when you talked to the deputies."

"He'd been drunk. He wouldn't have remembered." And even if he had, he would probably have lied to the police just to make Cain suffer. The old man would've gotten a kick out of seeing him stuck in jail for as long as it took the cops to sort things out.

If they managed to sort it out at all.

"You didn't want to try explaining something like that to the cops?"

"If they'd questioned him, he'd have made me pay, one way or another."

The skin around her eyes contracted. Not quite a full flinch, but enough. "I see."

"Don't do that."

"Do what?"

"Feel sorry for me. I chose to stick around here with him. I could have left almost any time I wanted."

"So why *did* you stick around?"

He changed the subject. "Are the cops questioning anyone else about Ariel Burke's pregnancy?"

"Your leaky old rowboat didn't spill that information?"

"Just wondering who'll get railroaded this time. She have a boyfriend?"

Sara didn't answer, but he was beginning to understand what her expressions and physical tics meant. Her eyes narrowed slightly. That meant he was right. Ariel Burke's boyfriends—

current and ex—would be getting a visit from the Ridge County Sheriff's Department.

"You said Renee had a secret boyfriend." Sara leaned forward. "And she never told you anything about him? Never hinted who it might be? Clearly she considered you a friend. Donnie said Renee told him you were one of the few people she felt she could trust."

The burning sensation returned to his eyes. He made a show of rubbing his forehead to hide his reaction to her words.

"You didn't know that, did you?" she asked gently.

Apparently she was learning to read him, too. "I knew she trusted me, or she wouldn't have bothered with me at all. Renee showed you how she felt by the things she did, not the things she said."

"So the father of her baby might not have realized how much she cared for him. She might never have told him."

He looked up sharply. "She slept with him. If he knew anything about her at all, he'd have known exactly how much she loved him. She wasn't the kind of girl who did something like that without it meaning everything."

"So you and she never…"

"No. We never." He managed a rueful smile. "Not from my lack of trying. But she didn't love me. Not like that. She told me I didn't love her, either. Not the way I would love the right person someday."

"She was a romantic."

"Yeah, she was."

"Do you know when she met the guy she loved enough to sleep with?"

"I think she was already in love with him before she and I ever became friends." He'd forgotten that fact, he realized. Mostly because she'd never come right out and said so, but it hadn't taken long to realize she was nursing a secret passion for *someone.*

He'd just never learned who that someone was.

"I kept asking her, if she and Mr. Right were so meant for each other, why couldn't she tell me who he was? She'd just give me this serious look and tell me love was complicated and I'd understand someday." He looked up suddenly at Sara, realizing how much he'd revealed to her with very little effort on her part. "You're good, Detective Lindsey. Very good."

Her lips curved slightly. "It helps that you're not my prime suspect."

"Do you have a prime suspect?" he asked, curious.

"Not for Renee's murder."

"What about for Ariel's? A boyfriend, maybe?"

"I need evidence before I start naming suspects."

"I heard she was a cheerleader."

"That's right." Sara nodded.

"Renee wasn't anything like that. She wasn't one of the popular girls. Too quiet for that."

"I remember."

"She had long brown hair. What about Ariel?"

"Blond and cut short for cheerleading."

He looked at her through narrowed eyes. "So, if you were a profiler looking at the two victims, you wouldn't see much in common."

"Except they were pregnant and killed by ligature strangulation at Crybaby Falls."

"Copycat?"

She gave him a considering look. "Maybe. Though a real copycat might have done his killing three days ago on the actual anniversary. To make a statement, I mean."

He rubbed his jaw, realizing at the scrape of his beard against his palm that he hadn't shaved that morning. Falling back into old habits, he thought with an inward grimace. He needed a haircut, too. And he'd been throwing on any old pair of jeans in the morning since he'd been assigned this case, grabbing any ratty T-shirt and ignoring the scuffs on his boots rather than taking care to present a neat and polished outward appearance the way the Army had taught him to do.

Falling back into old habits he'd thought he'd put behind him.

"What are you thinking?" she asked curiously.

He shot her a sheepish grin. "Believe it or not, I was thinking that since I came back here to

Purgatory, I've been letting myself go. Forgetting to shave, not spit-shining my boots, waiting too long to do the laundry—"

To his surprise, she laughed. "Reverting to your sloppy high-school self, you mean?"

He liked her laugh, the low, throaty sound sending a pleasant rippling sensation down his spine. He smiled back at her. "I guess maybe so. Don't want to let it go too far, though."

"I had trouble leaving my parents' house to come back here this afternoon because my mama cooks for me every time I go there." She shot him a sheepish look. "My old room still looks the same, even. I could move right back in like nothing has changed."

"But everything's changed."

"Not all for the worse," she said after a brief silence.

"No, not all," he agreed.

She dropped her feet to the floor. "I'm going to make coffee. Want some?"

"Sure. I take it black."

She slanted a smiling look at him. "So do I."

They settled into a surprisingly comfortable silence while Sara brewed the coffee in the adjacent kitchen. The coffeemaker looked ancient, apparently a fixture that had come with her inherited cabin. But the strong, hot brew she delivered into his hands a few minutes later left nothing to be desired. "Good coffee."

"I was surprised myself," she said with a glint of humor as she sat across from him again, cradling her mug between her hands. "I guess new isn't always improved."

"You think I should give up this case and let the cops handle it."

She looked at him over the top of her cup, her dark eyes hard to read. "As much for your own sake as for the good of the investigation."

"I'm not giving up. I can't."

She lowered the cup, cradling it in her palms on her lap. "I didn't think you would."

"So why don't we work together instead of against each other?"

Her brow furrowed. "Together?"

Clearly not an idea she cared for, he realized

with a flicker of dismay. He supposed it was one thing to let him into her house and give him a cup of coffee, but another thing altogether to trust him to have her back in an investigation.

Especially the investigation of a murder he was once suspected of committing.

"Never mind," he said as the silence stretched between them. He set his coffee cup on the low table between them. "Thank you for the coffee. I'll be on my way."

She rose with him, following him to the door. When he turned to look at her, she was frowning at him. "I didn't mean to hurt your feelings."

He almost laughed. "Don't worry yourself. My feelings are just fine." He gave a nod and headed out to his truck, a grin spreading over his face at the thought of her concern.

Imagine if she knew some of the things he'd endured growing up.

SARA'S CELL PHONE rang five minutes after Cain drove away. The number was a local one, not familiar. Not Cain's, as she'd hoped, given how lousy she was feeling about the way he'd left.

"Sara? This is Becky Allen. You remember, Jim Allen's wife? We talked at the party the other day."

"Of course," Sara replied, wondering how the coach's wife had gotten her cell phone number.

Becky's next words answered that question. "You mother was nice enough to give me your number. I just wanted to check in with you after what happened at the party the other night. That terrible news just—well, I was just thinking it was so much like what happened to Donnie's sister all those years ago, and hitting so soon after the anniversary of Donnie's death…" Becky trailed off to a soft sigh, as if she couldn't figure out how to say what she wanted to convey.

Torn between irritation at the reminder of all she'd lost and guilt at feeling irritated by honest attempts to be thoughtful, she pasted a smile on her face, though no one was there to see. "I'm fine, Becky, thanks. You're sweet to worry about me, but it's the Burkes who can probably use everyone's concern these days."

"It's just so horrifying. I'm to the point I don't even want my own child to go to Purgatory High now."

"You can't possibly have any kids in high school yet," Sara protested, thinking of how young the coach's wife had looked at the party.

"I do. Jeff is already a senior."

"Wow. Where's the time gone?"

"Beats me," Becky said with a rueful laugh. "Listen, I've got to get back to work, but if you're going to stick around town for long, you should come have dinner with Jim and me. Jim thought so much of Donnie, and I know he'd want to have you over before you head out of town. How long are you staying?"

"Awhile, at least," she answered carefully, thrown by the invitation. While Donnie had been one of Jim Allen's star players on the Purgatory High School baseball team, teachers and students hadn't made a habit of socializing. It wasn't as if they were old friends looking to catch up.

Then again, she hadn't been living in Purgatory since she was eighteen years old, and it was a pretty small town. Both Becky and Jim had been Purgatory students themselves, several years ahead of her and Donnie. Class president, homecoming queen, Miss Purgatory High— all those milestones that constituted royalty in a small town. Jim had been the baseball star, the good-looking kid who'd played a couple of years in triple-A before giving up the dream of a professional career and coming back to marry his high-school sweetheart.

No wonder they both kept themselves looking good. They had a reputation to live up to. Royalty didn't get to let themselves go.

"I'll get with Jim and we'll make a date," Becky said brightly. "Talk to you soon."

Bemused, Sara hung up the phone and turned to survey the cabin, thinking about Becky's question. How long *was* she planning to stick around Purgatory?

CAIN'S GRANDMOTHER'S cabin was only minutes away by truck, a vivid reminder of how small Purgatory, Tennessee, was compared to Atlanta. He could get everywhere in Ridge County faster than he could have driven from his apartment to the construction company where he'd worked. And many places on foot, too, for that matter. Sara's recently inherited cabin, for instance, was just a short hike over the hill from where his Airstream was parked on Mulberry Rise.

He wondered what she was doing right now.

When he pulled up beside the Airstream, he saw his grandmother's old station wagon was gone. A glance at his watch suggested why—it was nearly five on a Sunday, which meant she and the girls had gone to church for the evening services. For a woman some of the more superstitious folks in these parts considered a white witch, his grandmother had always been strict about her church attendance, and if he'd been home when she set out, she might have given him a stern talking-to about his own backsliding ways.

He smiled at the thought as he climbed the stairs to his trailer, but his smile faded when he spotted a plain white envelope tucked into the space between the door and the frame.

As he started to reach for it, his recent training kicked in, and he withdrew his hand, giving the envelope a quick once-over. Digging in his jacket pocket, he pulled out his multiblade knife, withdrew the small set of tweezers tucked into the handle and clamped the envelope between the two small tongs, tugging it free of the door.

There was no writing on either side of the envelope, and the flap hadn't been sealed shut. Using the hem of his T-shirt to hold the envelope, he pulled up the envelope flap with the tweezers and took a look inside.

A piece of plain paper sat tucked inside the envelope. Cain pried it out with the tweezers and read the three typewritten lines.

Look in your grandmother's woodbin. Imagine what might have happened if I'd called the police.

Alarmed, Cain slid the note back into the envelope and carried it with him down the steps and around his grandmother's cabin. Near the river-stone chimney sat his grandmother's woodbin, where she and the girls stored their firewood. He used his T-shirt to lift the lid of the bin and looked inside.

At first, he saw only pieces of chopped wood stacked neatly inside. But a closer look revealed the edge of a plastic bag peeking out from between a couple of the logs. He reached down and moved aside the top piece of wood, staring in mounting dismay at what lay beneath.

A quart-size resealable plastic bag nestled amid the pieces of wood. Inside the bag, four smaller clear plastic bags were tucked together. Each of the smaller bags contained dozens of crystals the color of pale champagne.

Around these parts, he knew, there was only one thing those crystals could possibly be.

Leaving the bag where it lay, he pulled out his cell phone and hit the first number on his speed dial.

Alexander Quinn answered. "We do get days off, you know."

Under any other circumstance, Cain might have smiled at his boss's dry response. If anyone in the world didn't know the meaning of the term "day off," it was Alexander Quinn. Cain wasn't sure the man even slept.

But Cain wasn't in the mood to smile at the moment.

"I've got a problem," he said into the phone, his gaze still fixed on the bag of crystals inside the woodbin.

"What's up?" Quinn was instantly all business.

"I came home to a note stuck in my door frame that told me to look in my grandmother's woodbin and be glad nobody had called the police."

"And what did you find?"

"I can't be sure until we test it, but I think I'm looking at about fifty grand's worth of crystal meth."

Chapter Eight

Sara pulled up in front of the small, neat cabin on Mulberry Rise, her gaze slanting toward the silver Airstream trailer parked beside it as she put her truck in Park and let it idle a moment.

She hadn't planned to come here when she'd left the house that morning, but when the turn-off to Mulberry Rise loomed in her windshield, dead ahead, her hand had flipped the turn indicator and she'd headed up the mountain as if following some inexplicable instinct.

Cain Dennison was trouble. He'd always been trouble, he probably always would be trouble, forever and ever, amen. But she'd spent a whole night feeling terrible about turning up her nose at his offer to work with her to find Renee Lindsey's killer, so the least she could do was apologize for being so blunt with him.

Except why should she apologize? She hadn't changed her mind—his history with Renee Lindsey made him the wrong person to be leading The Gates' investigation in the first place. She wished she could go ask his boss why he'd made such a confounding decision.

Then again, she didn't exactly see her own connection to Renee as a deal breaker, did she? She'd been married to Renee's brother. She couldn't imagine her mother-in-law, Joyce, would be happy to hear that she was delving into Renee's murder, either.

As she reached for the gearshift to put her car in Reverse, the front door of the cabin opened and a wiry woman in her seventies stepped onto the shallow stoop. Her gaze turned toward Sara's truck, and she offered a placid smile of greeting.

Stifling a sigh, Sara left the car in Park and shut off the engine. She could hardly rebuff two people in the same family within a twenty-four hour period, could she?

Lila Birdsong wrapped her shawl more tightly around her shoulders as a chill autumn wind blew through the trees, stirring her wispy white hair around her pretty, heart-shaped face. "Sara Dunkirk. Ain't seen you in ages."

"No, ma'am. I've been down in Alabama for a long while."

"My grandson tells me you're back for a spell. Thinkin' of stayin'?"

Sara wasn't sure how to answer that question. "I'm just thinking, at the moment," she said finally, managing a smile. "Is Cain here?"

Lila shook her head. "He headed out early so he could drop the girls off at the high school before going to the office."

"The girls?"

"Mia and Charlotte Burdette. Daughters of a cousin of mine who's smack in the middle of a mess." Her tone darkened. "I took those poor girls in to keep them out of the DCS."

Sara nodded, understanding. Like many child-welfare agencies, the Tennessee Department of Children's Services was perennially over-worked protecting children from unsafe or abusive home situations. Keeping children out of the system when possible was the better choice.

"How old are they?"

"Sixteen and seventeen." Lila grinned at Sara. "I reckon they were happy enough havin' Cain drive them around."

Sara could imagine. Even though she'd been in love with Donnie Lindsey since middle school, she hadn't been immune to the bad-boy appeal of Cain Dennison. He'd possessed the feral charms of a wild creature, both beautiful and dangerous.

He still did, she thought, remembering her first look at him in years, standing outside her hiding place at Crybaby Falls. Dangerous, yes, but also sexually exciting.

Lila's smile widened as she beckoned Sara to join her. "I've just brewed up some coffee. Come on in and tell me what's on your mind."

The last thing she intended to tell Cain Dennison's grandmother were the thoughts that had just flashed through her mind, but the offer of coffee sounded good. She followed Lila into the warm cabin and sat in the chair Lila waved toward.

"Cain ought to be back soon enough. He was just going into town for an early meeting." Lila returned to the table with a battered old stovetop percolator that had seen better days. But the fragrant, steaming brew she poured into a couple of stoneware mugs smelled like heaven.

"Thank you." Sara picked up the cup and took a sip. It was hot and strong, the way she liked it.

"No cream or sugar," Lila commented with a smile as she opened the refrigerator that stood in a corner near the table. "Must've been raised by a strong man."

Sara laughed. "Yes, but it was my mother who taught me to like coffee black. My father likes his cream and sugar."

Lila laughed with her as she retrieved a carton of cream from the refrigerator and poured a dollop into her coffee. "I reckon I do, too."

"Cain likes his coffee black, too," Sara commented as Lila returned to the table.

The older woman's eyebrows ticked upward. "So he does. I didn't know you knew him that well."

"I don't, really." Sara avoided Lila's gaze. "I just had coffee with him recently, that's all."

"Hmm," was all Lila said.

Squelching the urge to fill the suddenly uneasy silence, Sara sipped her coffee and wondered why she hadn't turned down Lila's offer of coffee and gone on her way.

"I was real sad to hear about your husband's passing," Lila said a moment later. "And real glad to see you're doing good now. I heard you were banged up pretty bad."

"I was. I'm lucky to be alive."

"Lucky," Lila murmured, as if she disagreed.

"Well, lucky, I guess, that your grandson was hiking the gorge that night. If he hadn't found me when he did, I don't think I'd have survived."

Lila nodded and looked up, her sharp brown

eyes meeting Sara's gaze. "I don't think things in this world happen randomly. Do you?"

"I don't know," Sara admitted. "Sometimes things in life seem very random."

"Seem," Lila said with a nod. "That's a real good word. I reckon many things seem to be what they ain't."

"And sometimes they simply are what they are."

"Life ain't simple," Lila disagreed. "Do you know how unlikely it was for my grandson to be there in the Black Creek Gorge so late at night? He hadn't been in Purgatory in years."

"Why *was* he back here that night?" Sara asked, curious.

Lila smiled over her coffee cup. "He'd just left the Army and gotten himself a good job in Atlanta. It was supposed to start the next Monday, but for the first time in years, his time was his own. So he came home. To see me, I imagine, but I think he really came to pay his respects."

To Renee, Sara thought. Three years ago, the day after Sara's car accident, had been the fifteenth anniversary of her passing. "He would have gone to Crybaby Falls," she said quietly.

"Yes."

"But that doesn't explain why he was at the Black Creek Gorge."

"No, it don't," Lila agreed.

Sara waited for her to say more, but Lila just sipped her coffee.

"I wish I'd had the chance to thank him," Sara said when the thick silence filling the kitchen became too uncomfortable.

"I don't reckon he thought he needed thanking," Lila said thoughtfully. "It ain't his way."

"It needs sayin', anyway," Sara said, smiling a little self-consciously as she heard her accent slip into the old, familiar intonations of her mountain upbringing. She'd been away from the hills for years, but some parts of her past a person could never really leave behind.

The sound of a vehicle coming up the mountain road seeped through the cabin's walls, drawing Lila's gaze to the front door. "I guess that'll be Cain comin' back."

Sara felt her heart speed up, just a notch. Just as it might if she heard a black bear approaching in the woods, she reminded herself sternly.

Beautiful but dangerous.

The thud of footsteps on the stoop outside gave her just enough time to steel herself for his entrance. He came through the door, filling its frame almost completely, as if to amplify for Sara's already pounding heart just how big he'd become in adulthood, how tall and broad-shouldered. As a boy, he'd been lean, wiry almost, but his time in the Army had clearly added brawn and power to his build that his time away from the service hadn't erased.

His storm-gray eyes met hers, wary and watchful. "I thought that was your truck outside. Has something happened?"

"No. I just wanted to talk to you." She glanced at Lila, not ready to say the things she needed to say to him in front of an audience.

He nodded at Sara before bending to give his grandmother a quick kiss on the top of her head. The gesture of affection made Sara's heart contract.

"The girls are safely at school, although they tried to convince me to let them ditch and take them in to work with me," Cain told his grandmother. The smile in his voice made Sara look up in time to catch a toothy grin so infectious, she felt her own lips curving up at the corners. "They said it would be educational. Sort of a 'take your grandmother's wards to work day.' I told them no, of course. Because education's a privilege."

Sara could tell by his intonation that his final words were a well-learned quotation, no doubt from his smiling grandmother.

"And so it is," Lila said, giving him a swat on the back as she rose to her feet. "It was a real pleasure havin' coffee with you, Sara Dunkirk, but I'm afraid I've got chores to get to, so I'll leave you with Cain."

Cain waited until his grandmother disappeared into the next room before he spoke, his tone low and urgent. "Has there been another murder?"

She looked up at his worried expression. "No, I told you, I just came to talk to you."

His gaze went from worried to wary. "I thought you already said about all there was to say."

"That's what I wanted to talk about." She nodded toward the back door, and he opened it, letting her go out ahead of him.

Outside, the wind had kicked up, swirling fallen leaves around their feet. Sara had forgotten, in the toasty warmth of the cabin, how cold the fall air had become. Winter was coming to the hills, sooner than she liked.

Hugging herself for warmth, she looked up at Cain, finding him no less imposing in the wide open than she had in the close confines of his grandmother's cabin. His expression was shuttered, forbidding, sparking an unexpected quiver in the pit of her stomach.

"You don't want me investigating Renee's

death," Cain said. "I plan to do it, anyway. Not sure anything more needs saying."

"I don't want you involved in the investigation because there's no way for you to not be in the way."

His eyebrows rose a notch, and she realized how badly she'd just expressed what she was trying to convey.

"I just mean—"

He cut her off. "I know what you mean."

"No. You don't." She caught his arm as he started to turn away.

He looked down at her hand, then up at her, his eyes narrowed. Beneath her fingers, his arm felt as hard as mountain granite but as hot as the coffee cup she'd cradled earlier between her cold fingers. The combination of unflinching strength and fiery vitality sent a different sort of quiver racing through her, straight to her sex.

She stared up at him, both confounded and aroused. His eyes narrowed further, as if he read her emotions and found them just as confusing.

"I know you're not going to believe me, but I'm as worried about you as I am about the case." As she said the words, she realized they shouldn't be true. The case should be everything. In some ways, indirectly, Renee Lindsey's murder was why she'd decided to come back to Purgatory at all. Her death had been a profound part of Donnie's life, of their marriage and, she feared, of his death, as well. Solving her murder might answer the questions that still kept her up at night, quiet the fears and doubts that robbed her of her peace.

She should care more about finding Renee's killer than she cared about Cain Dennison's well-being. He'd offered to help her with her investigation, and he certainly had more direct knowledge of Renee's last days than she did.

Why wasn't she willing to use him the way he'd so willingly offered to be used?

"Why?" he asked, echoing the question hammering in her head.

"You were run out of town by her death," Sara

said, though she knew that answer wasn't adequate. "I don't want it to happen again."

"Why would you care?"

"Fine," she said. "I think you complicate the case too much. You'd make it hard for people to trust my motives if they knew we were working together."

"Now we get to the truth," he murmured.

But Sara knew it wasn't the truth. Not all of it. Not by a long shot.

What the hell was going on with her? She'd been a widow for three years, not all of those spent in mourning black. She'd been asked out on dates, had even gone on a few, but not once, not a single time, had she thought of those men as anything but casual dinner companions. Not even a spark of attraction had fluttered low in her belly with any of those men, and she'd come to accept, even cherish, the idea that she was wed to her husband for life, dead or alive.

How could Cain Dennison, of all people, make her feel as if that part of herself might still be alive and kicking?

"We don't have to be open about our…collaboration," he said when she said nothing more. His lips curved in a wicked smile. "We can be secret partners."

The low, almost seductive tone of his voice snaked through her like a lightning strike. She felt the thunderous aftermath low in her belly, a shudder of raw, unwelcome need.

Agreeing with him would be the worst possible decision she could make. She knew it bone deep. But when she opened her mouth to speak, the word that spilled from her lips was "Okay."

He gave her another narrow-eyed look, as if he suspected she was joking. "Okay?"

This was her chance to back out, she thought. Laugh and agree that she'd been joking.

But she couldn't, she realized. No matter what kind of fluttery things he did to her insides just by being Cain Dennison, he was right about one thing. He did know more about Renee Lindsey's final days than anyone else in Purgatory, save the killer himself. If she was serious about getting to the bottom of Renee's murder, she needed his help.

"Okay," she repeated, more firmly. "You're right. I need your help. And, frankly, you could use mine, as well."

"I need you, do I?" His smile made her heart flip-flop.

She had to get a hold of herself, and soon, she thought, before their secret partnership made her spontaneously combust and make a big mess all over his grandmother's front yard. "You do. I have access to people who, right or wrong, aren't gonna give you the time of day, much less any useful information. I'm the daughter of the primary detective on the case eighteen years ago, and I'm good friends with the deputy who's running the new murder case." As she continued speaking, drawing on her professional credentials, some of the sexual tension that had stretched her close to the snapping point began to ease, and she started to think she could make this secret partnership work after all.

Then he touched her. It was nothing but a brief

brush of his fingertips along the length of her arm, but it burned through her like a wildfire.

"You won't regret this," he said.

She had a feeling he was dead wrong about that.

SARA LINDSEY LOOKED around his small, sparsely furnished Airstream with a curious gaze, as if assessing him as she took in the decor. He'd come up wanting, he feared, if she judged him on his temporary abode. He'd done little to make it feel like home, mostly because he didn't want to become too used to the place.

He'd grown up in a ramshackle cabin not much larger than this tiny trailer, and for a long time, even after he'd joined the Army and expanded his horizons, he'd felt too small for the world around him. Too lacking, too unworthy of so much space, so much opportunity.

His father had taught him to think small, to expect the worst. Hell, the man had shown him some of the worst life had to offer, made him think it was all he'd ever have. All he'd ever deserve.

For two short years, Renee Lindsey had made him think differently. She'd liked him. Trusted him.

And he'd begun to dream.

"When Renee died," he said aloud, drawing Sara's gaze back to him, "I thought it was the end of my life."

Sara's dark eyebrows lowered, her brow creasing. "You must have loved her a lot."

"I did. More than I realized, I think." Waving her over to the small sofa that nearly filled the front end of the Airstream, he pulled a ladder-back chair from beneath his tiny kitchenette table and placed it across from her, taking a seat. "I don't think it was the hearts-and-flowers kind of love," he added, smiling at the thought. "Renee knew it, even before I did. She didn't need a lover."

"She already had a lover," Sara murmured. "She needed a friend."

He nodded. "I'd never really had one of those

before Renee. People tended to give the Dennisons a wide berth, and they weren't wrong for that."

"Your father had a difficult reputation."

"He'd earned it, fair and square," Cain said, trying to keep the bitterness from swallowing him whole. "Every bad thing you've ever heard about him was probably true. And a whole bunch of things you didn't hear."

Sara's gaze grew troubled. "That bad?"

"Worse."

She closed her eyes briefly, and he felt her pity like a cold touch.

"Don't do that," he said gruffly.

Her eyes snapped open. "Don't pity you?"

"I don't want it."

"Pity isn't an insult. It's just a feeling." She reached across the table. Touched his hand.

As her fingertips lingered there, cold against his skin, he felt a surge of raw desire so powerful it nearly swamped him. He drew his hand away before he lost his senses completely.

Sara pulled her hand into her lap and looked

down at the table. "If it makes you feel any better, I'm in awe of you, as well."

"Don't do that, either," he said gruffly. "Don't make me out to be some sort of tragic hero."

"Wouldn't dream of it." Her voice was bone dry.

A smile tugged at his mouth. "No, I suppose you wouldn't."

"I just mean, you're here and you're sane. I came from a great family. I had a great husband. A great life. And sometimes I feel as if I'm living in a world I don't even recognize anymore." She looked self-conscious as she tucked a loose strand of hair behind her ear, not meeting his gaze. He supposed she was no more used to talking about her feelings than he was, especially after being alone for nearly three years.

Then again, maybe she hadn't been alone. Maybe there'd been someone else after Donnie's death. Maybe a lot of someones.

He didn't like that thought. Nor did he like just how much he didn't like that thought.

"Where do you think I should start looking?"

Sara broke the thick silence that had begun to descend between them.

"For Renee's murderer?"

She nodded, meeting his gaze again. "You probably knew her better than anyone else, right? So where should I look?"

He licked his lips as the answer occurred to him, knowing she probably wouldn't care for what he was about to say. But she'd asked for his honest assessment, hadn't she? He owed her the truth.

"I think you should try to remember what happened the night of your accident," he answered.

As he expected, her brow creased into a troubled frown. "I'm not sure that's even possible. And more to the point, why would that be the place to start looking for Renee's killer?"

He voiced the suspicion that had been building since he found the crystal meth in his grandmother's woodbin. "Because I'm not sure your wreck was really an accident."

Chapter Nine

A flood of cold swallowed Sara's whole body as Cain's words sank in. She fought the strange paralysis with a shake of her head. "There was no evidence of tampering—"

"I don't know how it was done," he said. "I just think there's reason to believe whoever killed Renee would stop at nothing to keep his secrets."

She clasped her hands tightly in front of her, unnerved by the way they were suddenly shaking. "Nobody knows his secrets. The police don't have a clue who killed her. None of us do."

"Someone thinks it's possible for us to find out," he told her, his voice unusually subdued.

Leaning toward him, she lowered her voice, as well. "What's happened?"

Anger blazed in his eyes when they met hers. "Yesterday afternoon, when I got home from your place, there was a note tucked into my door frame. Plain envelope, no name. Inside was a typewritten note that said, 'Look in your grandmother's woodbin. Imagine what might have happened if I'd called the police.'"

Another chill washed through her. "What was in there?"

"About five hundred grams of crystal meth."

She stared at him. "What?"

"Street grade, if the guys at The Gates are right about it."

The Gates? He'd taken the drugs to work? Had he lost his mind? "You didn't turn it in to the cops?"

"Where they can stash it with all the other pounds of crystal meth they've got stored up from drug busts in these mountains while they haul me and my grandmother in for drug trafficking and send those two poor girls into the

DCS system?" He looked at her as if *she* were the one who'd lost her mind. "No, thanks. Quinn can get rid of it just as well as the cops, and nobody gets framed."

"What about fingerprints? Trace evidence?"

"The Gates can handle that, too," he said calmly.

She blew out a long breath, shaking her head. "You like to live dangerously. What if a cop had pulled you over on the way to the office?"

"I'd be in jail. Luckily, that didn't happen."

She had grown up in a household where the law was damned near sacrosanct. But would she have been so quick to call the police if she'd found herself in Cain's situation, with his family background?

Probably not, she had to admit. "The chain of evidence has been completely obliterated."

"We'll find some way to use anything we discover." He sounded less than hopeful.

"You don't think you're going to find anything, do you?"

"Nobody gets away with murder for eighteen

years if they go around making it easy for people to find them."

She couldn't argue with that point. Donnie had become increasingly obsessed with finding his sister's murderer in the months and years preceding his death, and he'd gotten nowhere, despite his intimate knowledge of her life, her personality and her circle of friends and acquaintances.

Whoever had killed her had done a good job of covering his tracks.

"Okay," she said finally, "I'll buy that. But how does this attempt at blackmailing you figure into my accident? I was the one who was driving. And believe me on this—I wasn't the one who was asking all the uncomfortable questions around Purgatory. That was Donnie. Anyone who wanted to put an end to his investigation would have gone after him, not me."

"He was with you in the car that night."

He had a point. "But I can't find anyone who knew we were going to be in Purgatory that weekend. When would someone have had the chance to do anything to tamper with the truck?"

"You were in Purgatory the night of the accident, Sara, and you don't remember where you went."

She realized what he was implying. "You think we saw or heard something that very night."

He nodded slowly. "It's possible. Maybe even likely." He leaned toward her, the legs of his chair scraping closer. The warmth of his body washed toward her, tempering the cold that lingered in her limbs. "You want to remember what led up to the accident, don't you?"

She stared at him, realizing with dismay that she wasn't sure she knew the answer. She'd spent the past three years telling herself, telling everyone, that not remembering what happened was worse than remembering she was at fault. But was that true? Wasn't it easier not knowing? If she didn't know what happened, then there was still a chance she hadn't caused her husband's death.

What if she remembered everything and erased any hope that she wasn't at fault? Could she live with that knowledge?

She pressed her hand to her mouth. Her fingers trembled against her lips, to her dismay.

Cain reached across the remaining space between them to touch her hand, gently tugging it away from her face. "I know it must be scary."

"What if I—" She stopped short, unable to say the words.

"What if you didn't?" he countered, his voice warm. "What if someone tried to kill you and Donnie that night? Don't you want to know? Don't you want justice, if that's the case?"

His callused fingers, warm against her skin, had an unexpected calming effect on her trembling limbs. Strange, she thought as she looked up to meet his gaze, considering how his earlier touch had set fire to her blood. "Of course I do."

"Have you ever tried to remember?"

She stared at him, pulling her arm away from his grasp. "What kind of question is that?"

"I mean, I know you've probably tried to remember. Have you ever gone to someone for help recovering your memories?"

"If you're talking about hypnotic regression, I don't buy into that hokum," she said flatly. "There's a reason why it's not admissible in court."

"I'm talking about hypnosis to relax your mental barriers against remembering what happened. If you did hear or see something, your mind may not want to remember what it was. Maybe it's too painful."

Like doing something that ends in your husband's death? She looked down at her hands. "The doctors said it's possible I'll never remember. And after so much time, they're probably right."

"Did they say there was a physical reason why you couldn't remember? A brain injury?"

"I was in a coma for two weeks."

"But that was medically induced, right? Not a result of your head injury?"

She looked up at him, appalled. "How the hell do you know that?"

He looked apologetic. "It was part of the information your mother-in-law gave Quinn when she hired The Gates to look into her children's deaths."

Of course, she thought. Her parents would have thought nothing of telling Joyce Lindsey the details of Sara's condition. After all, as Donnie's mother, she'd have been considered family.

And Joyce, apparently, thought nothing of sharing Sara's personal medical information with strangers at a detective agency.

"Was Mrs. Lindsey wrong? Is there a medical reason you don't remember anything from that night?"

Swallowing the despair rising in her throat, she shook her head. "No. The doctors told me that my head injury was minor. Mostly scalp lacerations and abrasions. The CAT scan didn't show any damage to my brain."

"But when I found you, you were nearly delirious. Then you passed out cold."

She nodded, remembering the doctors' questions after she woke up. "They think it was a combination of emotional distress and pain. I had a couple of bad compound fractures, and the police think, based on Donnie's time of death, we were down there in that gorge for nearly four hours before you found us."

He winced. "I didn't know that."

"Four hours with a couple of compound fractures would be bad enough. Four hours aware that your husband flew through the windshield and was probably dead——" She shuddered, trying to push the thought from her mind, even now. No wonder she didn't want to remember that night.

"I wish I'd gotten there sooner." Cain touched her again, a light brush of his fingertips against her cheek. The potent urge to lean into his touch was so strong, she had to curl her fingers into the sofa cushion to keep from moving closer.

She couldn't stop a bleak laugh from escaping her raw throat. "I don't think it would have changed much. The coroner says Donnie was probably dead the moment he hit the windshield."

Cain dropped his hand. "Did he make it a habit? Not wearing his seat belt, I mean. Or did the belt fail?"

"That wasn't in the notes Joyce gave you?" she asked, immediately ashamed of the hard edge of her tone. It wasn't Joyce's fault that Sara couldn't provide the answers everybody needed.

"She didn't say," he answered quietly.

Of course she wouldn't have. One of Joyce's best—and worst—traits was her undying loyalty to her family. Renee and Donnie could do no wrong, no matter what they'd done.

She supposed Cain Dennison would find that trait a bit more appealing that Sara did. He'd grown up with a man who'd apparently found endless, unjustified fault in everything Cain had done.

But Cain hadn't had to live with that constant conflict between the truth and Joyce's unreasonable perception of her son. The only way to win Joyce's support would have been to agree with Donnie on everything. And Sara just wasn't wired that way.

"He usually wore his seat belt," she told Cain. "He was probably even more militant about it than I am. He was still in the traffic division, so he saw a lot of bad accidents."

Cain's eyes narrowed. "But he wasn't wearing it that night?"

"No. I don't know why he wasn't."

"So maybe you should find out."

Frustrated, mostly because she knew he was right, she scraped her hair away from her face and tried to come up with a reason to protest. But nothing came to mind. Nothing, at least, that would pass muster with her own sense of justice.

"Do you know anyone who does that kind of hypnosis?" she asked finally. "Is that something y'all do there at your fancy detective agency?"

He smiled at her question, the lines creasing his lean cheeks magnifying his masculine appeal until she felt her insides quiver. "I don't know of anyone at The Gates who could put you under hypnosis," he answered, "but I do know a tough old lady who can."

"ARE YOU TRAINED to do this?"

Sara's wary question didn't seem to faze Cain's grandmother. She slanted the younger woman a look of amusement as she pulled her old cane rocking chair closer to Sara's seat on the sofa. "Believe it or not, Sara Dunkirk, I am not uneducated."

"I didn't mean—"

"I just didn't get my education from your fancy schools," Lila added with a laugh. "My mother taught me what she called 'relaxing magic.' Not magic at all, of course, no matter what you may've heard 'bout us Birdsongs."

"I thought Birdsong was your married name."

Lila's eyebrows twitched. "I sent my man packin' the first time he came home drunk and tried to knock me around," she said with a hint of peppery heat in her voice. "Just like my daughter should've done. Though I reckon things happen as they ought, or Cain wouldn't be here."

Cain wasn't sure Sara, or anyone else, would find his presence in the world a compelling argument for his mother letting her husband knock her around, but he flashed his grandmother a smile, anyway.

"So you sent his last name packing at the same time?" Sara asked.

"No need to keep the name around if the man was gone." Almost as soon as she said the words, Lila sent a worried look toward Sara. "I didn't mean—"

"Different men, different situations." Sara waved off Lila's explanation. "If Donnie had been the kind of man to hit a woman, he'd have been gone the first time, too."

"Seems it's always the good ones that pass too soon," Lila said with a nod, sitting back in the rocking chair and giving a push with her legs. The chair started to gently roll back and forth on its rockers. The rhythmic cadence of floor creaks was part of the relaxation method, Cain knew from experience. He'd spent a lot of his adolescence right here in this room, with his grandmother rocking and humming, as she'd just begun to do. The sounds had done wonders to calm his agitated soul and help him survive the double shots of anger and fear that had dominated so much of his young life.

He could see his grandmother's rocking and humming start to have a relaxing effect on Sara, as well. She sank lower in the comfortable cushions of the sofa, her fisted hands releasing their death grip on each other and falling to either side of her legs.

"Do you know this song?" Cain's grandmother asked Sara, humming a few more bars of an old mountain ballad.

Sara began to hum along with Lila in a warm alto harmony. "'Darlin' Ginny,'" she murmured, a smile teasing the corners of her mouth. "My grandmother taught me that song before I could walk."

"Do you do the old-time ballad singin'?" Lila asked between hums.

"All by myself, no instruments?" Sara laughed. "Not if I can avoid it. I prefer singing harmony. Better suits my voice range."

Cain took his seat in the armchair near enough

to Sara and his grandmother that he didn't miss a word of their exchange but far enough back to make him a spectator rather than a participant. His gaze settled on Sara's face, watching the nuances of emotion play over her features as she and Lila conversed. She had a good face, he thought. Good bone structure, his grandmother would probably say, her code words for the kind of pretty that would last beyond the bloom of youth.

Sara was still young, but already he could see in the curve of her cheeks and the shape of her jaw what she would look like twenty years from now if life treated her well. She would still be a striking woman, able to command a man's attention as surely as she was commanding his now.

He didn't remember thinking of her that way when he knew her as a gawky teenager. She had still been aglow with lingering childhood, far too young and innocent for a boy who'd had to grow up way too soon.

But Sara had seen the darker side of life in

the intervening years, and it had toughened her. Carved a lot of the tenderness out of her, leaving sturdy bone and sinew in its place.

She continued to hum along with Lila, her eyes closing as she laid her head back against the sofa cushion. Across from her, Lila had pulled a half-knitted scarf from the bag of yarn and needles that hung from the back of the rocking chair, and the soft clack of knitting needles joined the symphony of chair creaks and ballad hums.

"I remember the night of your accident," Lila said quietly a few minutes later. "Fall had brung a chill to the mountains, and the trees was already startin' to turn colors."

"Yes." Without opening her eyes, Sara nodded. "It's always colder earlier up here than down in Birmingham at this time of year. You get spoiled down there, thinking summer's gonna last forever, and then before you turn around twice, you're shiverin' in your boots."

"Up here, you get a little warnin' that winter's

comin'," Lila agreed with a nod. "Reckon you didn't get no warnin' of the accident, did you?"

"I don't know." Sara's brow furrowed. "I don't remember."

"But you remember it was colder."

"I think so."

"The day had been a cold one, too. Cloudy like it was gonna rain, but it never did. Not 'til after dark."

"Donnie kept saying we should stay with his parents, but I wanted—" Sara stopped, her eyes snapping open. "I remember that conversation."

"Go on and sit back, sugar. Close your eyes again and just answer my questions, best you can." Lila's fingers never faltered on the knitting needles, and the rhythmic creaks of her rocking chair kept a steady cadence. "Your man wanted to stay with his folks, but you wanted somethin' different?"

"I wanted to get out of Purgatory," she said quietly, settling back against the cushions. "I'm just not sure why."

"Do you remember where you was havin' that

talk with your man? In the car? Over dinner in town?"

"Outside." A tiny crease formed over the bridge of her nose. "It was cold and windy, and there was just a hint of rain in the air. I told Donnie I wanted to leave Purgatory, but he said it was gonna rain and we ought to stay with his folks until morning." As she relaxed, Sara's voice had settled into a familiar Appalachian twang, sloughing off the veneer of years in the city to expose her mountain roots.

"Outside where?" Cain asked.

His grandmother shot him a warning look and he swallowed an epithet. He'd promised he'd stay a spectator.

His interjection didn't seem to bother Sara. She said, "It was a house, I think. We were parked on the street, so I guess maybe we'd gone to see someone."

"Who'd you go see?"

Sara's brow crinkled again. "Donnie had been making trips up here when he'd get a couple of days off in a row, lookin' up folks Renee had gone to school with. People who might remember something about her life at the time of the murder. He looked for Cain, but he couldn't track him down."

That's because he'd been in the Army, Cain thought. Lila would have told Donnie that much if he came around asking, though probably not how to reach him. Cain had been determined to steer clear of his father, and at the time he joined the Army, the old man was still alive.

"Can you take a look around you?" Lila asked quietly. "Just turn yourself around right there where you are, where you remember bein', and tell me what you see."

"It's a neighborhood," Sara answered after a moment of thought. "One of those subdivisions they've built out past the marble quarry. Right close to the city limits."

"Do you know anyone who lives out there?" Lila asked.

Sara's brows lifted. "The Allens, I think. Coach Allen and his wife bought a house out there right before we graduated. I remember because Becky Allen hired Donnie and a couple of other guys on the baseball team to come help them put up a fence to keep their dogs from wandering into the street." She opened her eyes and looked at Lila first, then Cain. "We went to see the Allens that night."

"Are you sure?" Cain asked.

Sara nodded. "I remember. Donnie wanted to talk to the coach because during her senior year, Renee had worked in the athletic department to get some internship credit for college. Donnie wanted to ask the coach if he remembered anyone coming to see Renee when she was working in the office."

"Did he?" Cain asked. He'd almost forgotten about Renee's internship with the athletic department.

"He said she mostly worked hard, kept to herself. Only person he saw her with, for the most part, was you."

He supposed that was probably true. Despite his aversion, at the time, for team sports, he'd come up with excuses to haunt the athletic office while she was working her shift, worried that some popular, good-looking jock would come along and snatch her away if he wasn't on guard.

After her death, he'd had far more painful things to remember about her.

"I wonder why the Allens never told anyone that we'd been by to visit that evening," Sara murmured, her brow creased with puzzlement. "I mean, after the accident, I know the sheriff's department went looking for witnesses. Surely they'd have tried to figure out where we were driving from."

"They did," Cain said with a nod. "They spread word they were looking for people who might have talked to you before the accident."

"And the Allens never came forward?"

"Not that I know of."

"I reckon you've done enough for today," Lila interjected, stilling the creak of her rocking chair and flashing Sara a smile. "But you just come on back whenever you want. I'll be right here, and we can commence rockin' and hummin' again."

Sara reached across to clasp Lila's hand. "You've given me somewhere new to look for answers. I don't know how to thank you."

"You just did, darlin'." Lila put her knitting back in the bag hanging from the rocker and looked up at them brightly. "I'm fixin' greens and pintos for lunch. Either one of you want to stick around for it?"

"That's very tempting," Sara said as she stood, sounding sincere, "but I really need to go see Coach Allen now."

"I'll go with you." Cain grabbed his jacket, kissed his grandmother's cheek and followed Sara to the door.

Chapter Ten

"What do you mean he's not here?" Sara's tone went from friendly to sharp in the span of a second, and considering the annoyance flashing in her dark eyes as she towered over the sweet-faced, middle-aged secretary in the Purgatory High School principal's office, it came as no surprise to Cain that the woman looked visibly shaken.

Sara might not be a cop anymore, but she could still be pretty damned intimidating.

"I'm sorry," the woman said when she finally found her voice, "but he and his assistant coach are in Nashville for a seminar on college-recruiting rule changes. There's so many nitpicky things you have to worry about these days to stay in compliance with the NCAA, our coaches like to stay on top of it. They'll be back here Wednesday morning."

"Maybe you could talk to Becky Allen," Cain suggested as he walked Sara back to her truck.

"She did call me, asking if I wanted to come over for dinner some night. It kind of took me by surprise, actually. It's not like we were great friends with her and the coach." She looked at Cain over the truck cab as she unlocked her door. "My stomach is growling. You hungry?"

"I could eat," he said with a smile, wondering if she'd given any thought to what kind of rumors might spread if people saw the two of them eating together in public.

"I heard there's a new Lebanese place in town. What's it called?"

"Tabbouleh Garden," he supplied.

"Right. Kelly Partlow told me about it." She pulled open her door and slid inside. When he'd settled in the passenger seat, she added, "In fact, isn't that where she ran into you last week?"

"It is." Cain smiled at the memory of Kelly's exuberant invitation to the alumni get-together. "She's a force of nature."

Sara laughed, catching Cain by surprise. It was a big, full-throated, uninhibited sort of laugh, the kind that made him want to laugh along. "She is definitely a force of nature. I sometimes wonder how she and I ever managed to become friends. We're so different."

"Are you? So different, I mean."

Her laughter faded as she turned her curious gaze toward him. "Yeah. Very different. She's a social dynamo—always wanting to be out and about. I prefer a night in, curled up in a chair reading a good book."

He smiled at the picture her words painted. "Literature or pop fiction?"

"Either. I'm not that picky." She buckled her seat belt and started the truck. "So, what's good at Tabbouleh Garden?"

"I had the falafel plate. It was excellent."

"There's a great little place in Birmingham with the most amazing falafel wraps," she said as she pulled out of the high school parking lot and headed the truck toward town. "Donnie never cared much for Lebanese food, but I couldn't get enough of it. Thank goodness one of my fellow detectives loved the place. I could talk him into going there to grab lunch at least once or twice a week."

"What did your fellow detective friend have to say about your leaving the police force?" he asked, curious.

"Garrett retired last year." She glanced at him as she pulled to a stop at a traffic light. "I think that was really the beginning of the end for me. I couldn't seem to connect with any of the other detectives on the squad, and I just didn't have the heart to stick around Birmingham after that."

"So you came home."

Her lips curved in a half smile. "I guess I did."

Tabbouleh Garden was doing brisk lunch-hour business, but Cain and Sara didn't have to wait long to get a table. The same pretty waitress who had served him and Darcy the previous week greeted them at the door and led them to a table in the corner of the room.

The waitress returned in a few minutes with the drinks they'd ordered—tea for him, lime-ade for her. She took a sip of the drink and gave a low moan of pleasure that sent fire blazing through his blood. "This is the best limeade I've had since Moakley's went out of business. Do you remember Moakley's?"

"Doesn't everybody?" He didn't add that, while he'd certainly heard of the old soda shop where all the kids in town had hung out after school, he'd never actually been there. He'd never had two dimes to rub together in those days. His father had refused to let him take an after-school job, demanding that Cain go straight home to take care of the chores. And going to Moakley's on the weekends was out as well, since his father had liked to keep Cain on a short leash.

"They had the best limeade. And they always put a slice of fresh lime in the cup." She laughed again, and the rippling sound was almost as sexy as her previous moan of pleasure had been. "My brother, Patrick, used to work at Moakley's during the summer, and whenever I was being a bratty pest—which was often—he'd swear the next time I ordered a limeade at Moakley's, he was going to put vinegar in the cup instead."

"Patrick was a couple of years ahead of me in school, I think."

She nodded, giving him a thoughtful look. "Donnie used to want to set him up with Renee, but Patrick already had one foot out of Purgatory by the time Renee was old enough for him to give her a second look. And Renee was such a homebody." She sighed, her fingers playing at the edges of the menu that sat on the table in front of her. "I'd forgotten that about her."

"She loved this town," Cain agreed. "I think her parents wanted her to go off to college and see the world, but she didn't want to leave Purgatory."

"I wonder how much her reluctance had to do with her mystery lover."

He'd wondered the same thing, especially after

her death. "I think Renee was just a mountain girl at heart. She used to love Crybaby Falls especially. She loved the whole romantic, tragic history of the place."

"The myth of the heartbroken Cherokee maiden, leaping to her death with her newborn baby?" Sara grimaced. "Tragic, maybe. Not sure I consider it romantic."

"Even after losing Donnie?" As soon as the words left his mouth, he kicked himself. What the hell was he thinking, asking something so personal? "I'm sorry. That was such a stupid question. Forget I asked it."

"It's okay." She reached across the table and covered his hand with hers. "I'm really a little tired of everyone tiptoeing around me these days."

"At least they don't run the other direction when they see you coming." He grimaced before the last word tumbled from his lips.

Sara's lips quirked at the corners. "Now who's pitying you?"

"That *was* pretty pathetic," he agreed as the waitress headed toward them with their orders.

"You sort of give off this vibe," Sara commented as she picked up her falafel wrap and gave it a considering look. "Like you're daring people to come close enough so you can snap your sharp teeth at them."

He frowned. "I do that?"

"A little." She took a bite of the wrap. Her eyes closed and she released a soft moan of satisfaction.

Heat flooded through his veins as he watched her enjoyment of the food and wondered how responsive she might be to other sensual pleasures. "Good?" he asked.

She nodded, her eyes opening to meet his gaze. "Really good."

"You might want to get your baklava to go," he suggested in a soft growl.

Her dark eyes widened slightly as she clearly understood his meaning. "Does it bother you?" she asked, a smile flitting across her lips. "My open display of pleasure?"

"Bother? Yeah, you could say that." He leaned closer, his heart pounding against his sternum. "But only because we're in public."

Her head cocked slightly. "We don't have to be. In public, that is."

"I think maybe we do." He sat back, fighting the urge to reach across the table and touch her flushed face.

She sat back as well, her expression thoughtful. "I don't have any expectations."

"You should. You're a woman who should always have expectations." He forced his attention to his own food, not ready to follow his baser instincts where Sara Lindsey was concerned. She might think she was a woman who could scratch a sexual itch without worrying about the consequences, but he could never see her that way.

Maybe that wasn't fair to her. Maybe he was being a sexist pig, putting her on some sort of pedestal she didn't ask to occupy.

Maybe he knew, deep down, that he wouldn't be able to walk away so easily himself?

"Do you have expectations?" she asked a few minutes later.

He looked up. "About you?"

"About anyone."

"No."

"Maybe you should, too."

He couldn't quell a wry smile. "I'll take your opinion under consideration."

"Your father really did a number on you."

He looked down at the remains of his lunch, no longer hungry. "I really don't want to talk about my father."

"I remember thinking how cruel he must have been to give you a name like Cain." She looked at him over the rim of her glass as she took a sip of limeade. "The original murderer."

"Well, since I was the only one who survived my birth—"

"You didn't kill your mother."

"He used to tell me, from the time I was old enough to understand, that I'd killed my twin brother in the womb and killed my mother coming out."

"The bastard." Her voice trembled with intensity.

"Yeah, well. Made me grow up tough, I guess."

"No kid should have had to listen to that kind of garbage."

No, he thought, no kid should. But on the whole, he'd preferred the words, which his blessing of a grandmother had taught him to ignore with the power of her love, than the beatings.

Not even Lila's love could prevent the bruises and broken bones.

Sara seemed to read his mood, changing the subject to college football and Tennessee's chances for a bowl bid. They concluded, by the time the waitress brought the check, that everything hinged on the sophomore who'd won the quarterback position in the preseason, and they left the restaurant debating the head coach's controversial choice.

What had been a sunny day was beginning to turn gloomy, storm clouds scudding eastward toward the mountains. "Rain's comin'," Sara said, and Cain managed a weak smile at the broadening of her accent. Back in town a few days and she was already picking up the mountain twang again. He was as guilty of that, he supposed, as she was.

You can take a fella out of the mountains...

"Cain?" Sara broke the silence a few minutes later as she turned off the main road and headed back up the mountain toward his grandmother's place.

"Yeah?"

"This is going to be a strange question, I know, but—do you think it's possible Coach Allen could have been the father of Renee's baby?"

"You're right. That's a strange question."

"I know. I just—don't you think it's strange he never came forward to tell anyone Donnie and I visited him the night of the accident?"

"Yeah, but it's a big leap to go from that to murder."

"I didn't say he murdered her." The first fat raindrops splatted against the truck windshield, and she turned on the windshield wipers. "But could he have been the person Renee was involved with?"

He gave the question a moment of thought. "Jim Allen wasn't much older than us students back then. I guess he was probably young enough to see a pretty eighteen-year-old coed as a viable sexual conquest. If he was the sort to cheat on his wife."

"Donnie once told me he thought Coach Allen and his wife were having trouble. He said he'd overheard something that made him wonder."

"I'm not sure you can base an investigation on something someone overheard nearly twenty years ago." Cain had been the focus of some nasty rumors in his day, based on not much less than what Sara was describing.

"I don't know how soon the cops are going to get a DNA profile on the baby Ariel Burke was carrying. But if it proves a familial match with the baby Renee was carrying—"

"We still don't have a DNA profile to match it to."

"So maybe we need to get our hands on Coach Allen's DNA."

Cain looked at Sara. She had both hands gripped tightly on the steering wheel, her gaze aimed forward toward the rain-slick road. But there was a trembling tension in her profile, reminding him of a hawk that had just spotted prey.

"What do you have in mind?" he asked cautiously. "Taking Becky Allen up on her dinner invitation?"

"If I have to. But there may be a way to get our hands on it while flying under the radar."

"Yeah?"

"Yeah." She turned to look at him, just a quick, vibrant gaze that sent a jolt of desire hurtling through his body. "How would you like to be my date to a charity hoedown?"

ON SATURDAY EVENING as she and Cain entered the Purgatory Community Center meeting hall, Sara discovered how seriously her mother and Rita Ellis had taken the charity fund-raiser's hoedown theme to heart. Normally, the community-center event hall was a bland, rectangular room with a dais at the back and two double doors at the front. Tonight, however, Ann Dunkirk, Rita Ellis and their little worker elves had transformed the place into the inside of a barn.

Bales of hay covered with colorful horse blankets lined the walls in the place of chairs, and the dais at the back, where the Meade family bluegrass band was tuning up for their first set, was adorned with stable doors, hitching posts and a variety of ropes and authentic leather tack.

"Yippie ki-yay," Cain murmured in her ear.

She shot him a warning glance. "It's a bit much, but my mother was part of it, so watch your mouth."

His only reply was a twitch of his lips.

She'd been finding it hard to drag her gaze away from him ever since he drove up to the cabin to pick her up for the dance. He looked downright edible tonight, in his Wrangler jeans, plaid shirt and leather jacket. He'd even worn a well-used John Deere cap that he'd folded and tucked into his back pocket when they entered the meeting hall.

He made redneck look pretty damned sexy.

And maybe if his good looks had been the end of it, she might have found him easier to resist. But he also possessed a solid core of decency he seemed so determined to hide from the world. In her work as a detective, she'd learned that a man's true self always found a way to peek through even the most well-crafted facade. All you had to do was wait for it to make an appearance.

Cain had shown his true self during lunch that day at Tabbouleh Garden, when he'd managed to make her feel wildly desirable at the same time he'd turned down her veiled invitation for no-strings sex.

You're a woman who should always have expectations, he'd told her.

If she thought she'd found him desirable before…

Forcing her gaze away from his deliciously

stubbled jaw, she spotted her mother talking to Nola Meade, a tall, rawboned woman in her early forties. Her strong, unadorned features were more handsome than pretty, her silver-streaked brown hair gleaming in the spotlights like warm honey. She held a mandolin tucked in the crook of her elbow like a baby and smiled as she spoke to Ann Dunkirk.

"Those the Meades?" Cain asked, nodding toward the stage.

"You've never heard them?"

Cain's mouth curved. "My tastes tend more toward Skynyrd and Marshall Tucker."

"Just promise you're not going to pull out your lighter and start hollerin' 'Freebird.'" She weaved her way through the milling crowds, heading for the dais. She could tell by the sudden buzz in the crowd that Cain was right behind her.

She should have warned her mother of her plans to bring Cain with her tonight, she realized when Ann's eyes narrowed at their approach.

Sara gave her mother a swift hug. "The place looks amazing."

"It's too much," Ann admitted, keeping her voice low. "Rita can be a bit exuberant."

"It's very festive," Sara insisted. She smiled up at Nola Meade. "Hey there, Nola. How're you doing?"

"Better'n I deserve, hon." Her brown-eyed gaze slid past Sara to snag on Cain standing close behind her. Sara didn't miss the spark of feminine appreciation in the other woman's eyes and couldn't blame her a bit.

"Nola Meade, this is Cain Dennison. Cain, this is Nola Meade, the best mandolin player in the hills."

"Not sure I'd go that far," Nola said with a broad smile. "Nice to meet you, Cain."

"Same here, Mrs. Meade."

"Oh, lord, just call me Nola, unless you want to make me feel old." Nola looked at Sara. "I was real sorry to hear about your husband."

"Thank you. It's been a tough few years."

As Nola made her excuses and turned back to

the work of setting up the stage for the family band, Ann caught Sara's arm and pulled her to one side of the stage, away from everyone else. She glanced toward Cain, who was waiting patiently by the stage, making a show of watching the Meades tune up their instruments.

"Do you really think it was a good idea to bring Cain Dennison?"

"He paid for his ticket like everyone else," Sara said quietly.

"Joyce still thinks he had something to do with Renee's death."

"Donnie didn't. He said that Cain was a good friend to Renee."

Ann glanced at Cain again. "Have you taken up with him?"

"Taken up with him?" Sara asked, shooting her mother a look.

Ann lowered her voice. "You know what I'm asking."

Sara sighed. "Cain and I both want to know what happened to Renee."

Ann's dark eyes narrowed. "It's not enough

that your daddy's come out of retirement with this terrible new case with the Burke girl—"

"Mom, it's what we do. You know that."

With a sigh, Ann slanted a look toward Cain again. "I think your date is trying to get your attention."

Sara turned and saw Cain watching her, his gaze urgent. She excused herself from her mother and crossed to where he stood. "What's up?"

"One of the coaches from the high school is here, and I overheard him telling his wife that Coach Allen had called in sick the past three days of school."

"Well, hell. I guess maybe that's why he hasn't returned any of my calls." She'd tried several times since Wednesday morning to get in touch with Coach Allen, with no luck. Nor had Becky Allen returned any of her messages.

"That probably means he won't show up to-night."

She frowned with frustration. Talking to Jim Allen had been her main reason for coming to this fund-raiser. In a crowd like this, she'd figured, she would have ample opportunities to get her hands on a discarded cup or plate that might contain enough of the coach's DNA to test against the profile of the baby Renee had been carrying at the time of her death.

Cain caught her elbow in his hand, tugging her with him toward the side of the room. If he was aware of the stares and whispers that followed them, he showed no sign of it. Once they were tucked between a bale of hay and a decorative haystack near a window looking out on the parking lot, he said, "Wonder if he's really sick?"

"You think he's faking it?"

"He has to know you're looking for him by now. You left enough messages."

"And he knows Donnie and I went to see him before the accident."

"Maybe he's afraid you've remembered something."

"All I remembered is being outside his house the night of the accident." Despite her attempts to recreate the relaxation techniques Lila Bird-song had used with her the other morning, Sara hadn't been able to uncover any more of her lost memories. "And he doesn't know I remember even that much."

Cain's hand stroked lightly along her arm, sending prickles of delicious heat darting through her. "Maybe not. But between Ariel Burke's murder and your sudden eagerness to talk to him—"

She looked up at him. "You think he might have killed Ariel as well?"

"I can't ignore the similarities in the murders." Cain lowered his voice to a near-whisper. "After we talked about Coach Allen the other day, I remembered something a guy told me back in high school. It was pure gossip, and I've learned not to spread gossip, since I was the focus of a lot of malicious lies in my own time."

"But?" she prodded when he paused as if he didn't want to continue.

"But back in high school, one of the guys in the crowd I hung with swore up and down that

there was a coach at the school who was sleeping around with some of the senior girls. What
if it was true? And what if that coach was Jim
Allen?"

Chapter Eleven

The start of the bluegrass set rolled through the hall almost as soon as Cain posed his question, enlivening the gathered crowd and raising the decibel level in the community-center hall so high that the only way Sara could have responded was with a yell.

Shooting him an apologetic look, she caught his hand and pulled him closer to the stage, where she joined with the crowd in clapping to the beat of the lively reel the Meade family had chosen to begin their set.

Next to her, Cain gave a shrug and started clapping along as well, his grin suggesting that, rock fan or not, he recognized the Meades could flat-out play. Nola's long fingers danced over the mandolin strings, coaxing riffs as fierce as any rock guitarist could hope for, and her older daughter, Tammie Jane, was defying physics on the banjo.

"They're good!" Cain said in her ear as the Meades finished the first song to applause and started straight into the next. The two younger girls, Tammie Jane and her sister, Dorrie, put down their banjo and fiddle respectively, heading to a pair of microphones. The girls began to sing in crystalline harmony to an old-fashioned two-step, and all around Sara and Cain, the fund-raiser attendees began pairing up to dance.

Sara turned to Cain and held out her hand. "Wanna dance?"

"I'm not much of a dancer," he warned as he caught her hand, pulling her flush to him. "But I'm up for a challenge."

Hiding a grin, Sara slipped her arm around his shoulders, settling her fingers in the silky waves of dark hair that brushed the collar of his denim jacket. He met her gaze, heat blazing in the depths of his gray eyes, and something at her core caught fire and started spreading until her whole body burned with excitement.

She'd been gawky as a teenager in most situations, but the one thing she'd always been able to do was dance. It was as if the music took over her body, erasing her gracelessness for the length of the tune.

Cain hadn't been kidding—he wasn't much of a dancer as they started, but he was a quick study, and he seemed to actually enjoy letting her subtly lead the dance, his gaze deepening each time her legs brushed his or their hips collided as she helped him through the steps that twirled them through the crowd.

But eventually, he took control, tugging her closer as his steps became more certain. Her heart pounded a quickened cadence in response, and by the time the song ended, she was nearly out of breath.

"You're a better dancer than you think," she said, trying to tell herself that it was the lively dance and not Cain's arms around her that had stolen her breath and jump-started her pulse. But she knew better.

It had been three years since she'd felt another heartbeat thud against her chest or fingers slide over her arm with sexual intent. And even though what she and Cain had just shared would seem, to others, nothing more than a lively two-step, she knew it was so much more.

It was a question. An invitation. The same invitation she'd so delicately hinted at a few days earlier over lunch. She saw it in his dark eyes, felt it in the way his hand lingered as he released her and stepped back.

What are we going to do about this thing between us? his eyes seemed to ask, and she didn't know the answer any more now than then.

All she knew was when the next song started, a plaintive ballad of love and longing, they reached for each other without question.

He felt solid. Real. For three years, she'd slept with a phantom memory of the man she'd loved since boyhood, awakening to an empty bed and living on the precipice of an aching chasm between what she'd had and what she'd lost. She'd grieved and, in many ways, moved on with her life.

But could she ever really love another man?

She and Donnie had been inseparable from the tender age of thirteen and she'd never doubted her decision to be with him, even during the stresses and strains that challenged every long-term relationship. Was it even possible to find that kind of love again?

Was she greedy to try?

It was stupid to be thinking about love in Cain Dennison's arms. They barely knew each other. What was stirring between their bodies had more to do with friction and hormones, not intimacy and affection.

But it had been a while since she'd let friction and hormones have their way. And she'd already made it plain to him that she'd be okay if whatever happened between them never led anywhere else.

She started to look up at him, to see if she

could read what he was thinking in those gunmetal eyes, but before her gaze reached his face, it snagged on a pair of newcomers who had just entered the community center. A hard chill washed over her, driving out the earlier heat, and she stiffened in Cain's embrace.

He pulled back to look at her. "What?"

As he started to turn his head to see what she was looking at, she tightened her grip on him. "Don't turn around. Joyce and Gary Lindsey just came in."

His expression shifted subtly from curiosity to dismay. He dropped his hands away from her body. "I'll go."

No, she thought, desperate to feel the heat again, anything but this disheartening blend of grief and shame. She grabbed his hand again and gave a tug. "There's a side exit between the punch bowl and that big scarecrow." Sara led him to the door and they slipped out into the darkness.

With the door closed, the music faded to a soft whisper of sound. Cain stepped away from her, withdrawing his heat and, with it, any shelter against the cold night air. Autumn was fading in the mountains, and winter was on the way, slithering like a promise of ice down her spine.

Sara wrapped her arms around herself and stared at him, not sure what to say or do now that she had him all to herself. What came out when she opened her mouth was a simple statement. "Winter's coming."

He held her gaze a long moment, as if trying to read what was going on behind her eyes. *Good luck,* she thought with bleak amusement. *Hell if I know myself.*

He reached out almost tentatively, as if he expected her to run at his first touch. When she didn't flee, he ran his hands gently up and down her arms as if to warm her. "You can go back in there now, you know. I'll go on home and Joyce doesn't even have to know I was here."

No, she thought again. She didn't know what she wanted to do, what was the right thing to do, but she knew she wasn't ready to let him leave. She lifted her chin, the decision made.

"You know small towns. It won't take a minute before someone tells her all about it."

"I don't want to make things harder for you. For either one of you."

Sara put her hand on his chest, flattening her palm over his heart. "I know."

He covered her hand briefly with his own, then started to step away, once more robbing her of his heat.

She caught his hand as the music coming from inside the hall changed again, to a plaintive lament that seemed to resonate in her own hollow chest. "Don't go."

"Sara—"

"Dance with me again."

He gazed at her in consternation, and she could tell he knew as well as she did that what she was suggesting was akin to lighting matches in a pool of gasoline. He closed his eyes briefly, as if struggling to make the right decision. When he opened them again, the fierce hunger in his gaze shot straight to her sex, setting her nerves vibrating like a tuning fork.

"You like to play with fire, don't you, Sara Dunkirk?" he murmured, tugging her close.

She melted into his embrace, letting the music work its magic on her normally graceless body. The tune was an old one, a mountain lover's plaintive song of love given freely and ripped away, and it made her feel equal parts melancholy and restless.

"This isn't why we came here tonight," he murmured, but he didn't make any effort to end the seductive glide of his body against hers.

"I know."

"You know how wrong I think this is," he added, not sounding as if he thought it wrong at all.

"It's a terrible idea," she agreed in a tone that suggested she, too, thought no such thing.

There was no reason to move from where they swayed under the weak golden light of the parking lot lamps, but before she realized it, they were swallowed by the shadows pooling near the cool brick wall of the community center. The music grew fainter, her pulse more thunderous in her ears as he pressed her into the wall. Though the bricks were cold and hard against her spine, all she felt was a fierce, shuddering thrill as he pinned her there with his long, lean body.

"If you don't want this, say so now," he whispered, his mouth inches from hers. His breath fogged the air between them, softening his features as he gazed at her with feral intent.

She curled her hand around the back of his neck and tugged him closer, lifting her face to him.

The first brush of his mouth to hers was exploratory, almost tentative. But when she darted her tongue against his upper lip, he twined his fingers with hers, trapping her hands against the brick wall as he slid his tongue over hers, drawing out her passionate response until she was gasping for air and sanity.

His mouth danced lightly across her jawline and over to her ear, nibbling lightly on the sensitive lobe before he whispered, "Let's get out of here." He released her hands and stepped back, leaving her feeling so boneless and weak she had to fight to keep from sliding down the wall into a puddle at his feet. Slowly, his gaze warm with sexy confidence, he held his hand out to her. "You coming?"

As soon as humanly possible, she thought, unable to stop a grin from spreading over her features at the naughty thought as she took his hand.

On trembling legs, she followed him across the parking lot to his truck.

WHAT THE HELL do you think you're doing, Dennison? Even as his heart pounded a fierce cadence of desire, his foggy brain struggled to regain control over his senses. He was driving Sara Lindsey back to her little mountain cabin as fast as his truck could go, to hell with traffic laws or anything resembling good sense. When he got there, he fully intended to strip her naked and explore every inch of that tantalizing body that had teased him all night beneath the layers of cotton and denim that had hidden it from his view. He was damned well determined to give her the best sex of her life.

Even if it was the worst idea he'd ever had in his whole sorry, misbegotten life.

"We're crazy, aren't we?" she asked, her tone still as breathless as it had been when she'd asked him not to leave outside the community center. He still heard the same tone of sexual excitement that he'd seen echoed in her dark gaze, but threaded through the arousal was a bleaker tone, a hint of fear and regret.

Tamping down the selfish urge to brush aside those reservations, he made himself slow the truck as it started the climb up the mountainside to her cabin. "Probably," he admitted.

She was silent long enough for them to reach the edge of her property. Cain pulled his truck in behind hers where it sat parked in the gravel in front of the cabin and shut off the engine. The ensuing silence felt heavy and thick with unspoken thoughts.

Sara turned to look at him, and any intention to do the right thing shot straight out of his brain when he saw the fire blazing in her hungry gaze. Reaching for her, he dragged her toward him, laughing helplessly as her seat belt foiled him.

Sara grappled with the clasp until it opened, freeing her to launch herself into his grasp in a tangle of arms and legs and searching lips.

He settled her between his body and the steering wheel, and if the wheel digging into her rib cage caused her any discomfort, she didn't show it, straining closer, her legs straddling his until he felt the fiery heat at the juncture of her thighs press intimately over his own straining erection.

Her thighs clenching, she rose slowly up his body and back down, deliberately creating friction between them. In the pale glow of the dashboard, he caught a glint of pure, wicked pleasure in her eyes as he was unable to stop a groan from escaping his mouth.

"That," she whispered against his mouth, "is what it feels like to discover you're still alive."

The sentiment behind her words stung him,

even as she slid her tongue against his, drawing him into another deep, heart-stopping kiss.

He struggled against the power of his lust for her, knowing she'd just told him something important and profound. Gently pushing her away until she winced a little at the press of the steering wheel against her back, he cradled her face and made her look at him. "What do you mean, to discover you're still alive?"

She made a face at him, impatience trembling in her touch as she tried to draw him back to her. "Nothing. I didn't say anything."

Wrestling with the selfish desire to take her at her word, he kept her from bending in for another kiss. "No, you said this was what it feels like to discover you're still alive."

With a growl of frustration, she slid away from his lap. He felt the absence of her soft heat like an ache, and not just the physical kind. A hollow sensation filled his chest as well, as if she'd removed something vital from inside him when she moved to her side of the truck cab.

"I haven't been with anyone since Donnie,"

she said. The words sounded hushed, as if spoken in the hallowed privacy of the confessional.

Cain had spent more time than he liked wondering if she'd broken her mourning with another man, but hearing her say the words aloud, he couldn't say he was surprised to learn she'd been faithful to his memory. She'd loved Donnie Lindsey since they were kids, and losing him couldn't have been something she'd get over easily.

"I guess it sort of felt like my life has been in limbo," she added when he didn't say anything. "I still felt married to a man who was dead. I guess it made me feel as if I was there with him, in death."

"And so this—" Cain waved his hand in the space between them "—is sort of like a limb coming back to life?"

She shot him a grin that was pure temptation. "Well, yes, if by limb you mean—"

He shushed her with two fingers against her lips. "When a limb comes back to life, there's usually a good bit of pain before it's all over."

The smile that curved against his fingers faded, and her eyes took on a serious light. "It's better than feeling nothing."

The sorrow in her voice echoed in his hollow chest, exacerbating the empty ache that had set up shop there when she drew away from him. He didn't let himself examine the sensation too closely, not ready to think about what it might mean that he felt her pain so keenly himself.

"I think we shouldn't do anything we can't take back," he said, steeling himself against any attempt she might make to change his mind. "I meant what I said the other day. You should always have expectations about something as important as who you sleep with."

"I meant what I said, too," she said quietly. "You should have expectations, yourself."

"Did you really expect anything good from what we were about to do?"

She turned her face forward to gaze through the front windshield at the darkened cabin. "I wasn't thinking about what happens next."

"You should. We both should."

"I'm not reckless by nature," she admitted. "I'm not used to feeling so out of control."

"Well, at the risk of stretching a metaphor until it snaps, a limb that's fallen asleep usually flails around a bit until all the feeling comes back."

She groaned softly on her side of the cab, slanting a look at him that made him smile for the first time since they'd stopped kissing. "Stop. You've definitely tortured that metaphor enough."

He couldn't stop himself from pressing the back of his knuckles against her cheek. "I'm done."

She caught his hand, her touch gentle but not inviting anything more than the small display of affection. "Thank you. And not just for putting the metaphor out of its misery."

"It's okay if you don't want to work together on this case anymore."

She shook her head. "We're adults. We can be professional, right?"

"Right," he agreed, even if there was a hint

of doubt still lingering in the back of his mind. He'd have to make their professional alliance work, even if it killed him, because if the past few weeks in Purgatory had proved nothing else to him, it was that he couldn't open nearly as many doors in this town as he needed to in order to get the answers he wanted. Sara was his key to a whole lot of information currently not available to him, and he didn't know if he'd get anywhere on the case without her.

"Will you stick around to see I get inside safely?" she asked, opening the passenger door. She shot him a sheepish smile that made his legs tingle a little. "You can take the cop out of the big city…"

He grinned. "I've got your back, Detective."

She walked slowly up the stairs to the front door, her body swaying slightly with each step, as if she could still hear phantom strains of music in the cold night air. She turned at the top of the porch and gave a little wave. He waved back, his chest squeezing into a hot, tight knot at the almost girlish vulnerability he glimpsed in her moonlit features.

He waited until she unlocked the cabin door and slipped inside before he started the engine. When the lights came on inside the cabin, Cain put the truck in Reverse and started to pull out.

Suddenly the front door opened and Sara hurried out, waving frantically as she ran down the stairs.

Cain jammed the truck into Park and rolled down his window as she hurried up to his door. "What's wrong?"

"Someone broke into the cabin and trashed the place," she said, fear mingling with anger in her blazing dark gaze. "And I think they took all the notes I've made on the case so far."

Chapter Twelve

The large front room of the small cabin was a mess. Sofa cushions had been ripped up and tossed around, the stuffing covering the hardwood floors like the aftermath of a fiberfill snowstorm. The sheer, back-breaking work it was going to take just to get the cabin back to where she'd gotten it over the past couple of weeks was enough to make Sara want to cry.

The damage the intruder had inflicted to photographs and mementos that couldn't be replaced, however, made her seething mad.

"That's the only photograph I have of my great-grandmother Dunkirk," she told Cain with a wave toward the black-and-white photo that had been pulled from its smashed frame and ripped into three pieces. "That broken vase there was made by my uncle Cyrus shortly before he went to Vietnam and died in battle."

Cain remained silent as he looked around the room, taking in the destruction. After a moment, he turned and put his hand on her cheek. "I don't even know what to say to you."

Despite her earlier determination to keep their relationship on a professional footing, she didn't resist when he pulled her into his arms. Pressing her cheek against the solid heat of his chest, she let herself have a quiet moment of mourning for what she'd lost that couldn't be replaced.

But after a minute, she lifted her head and squared her shoulders. "My guess is that what happened here is connected to our investigation."

"Maybe not. Maybe some meth head broke in looking for money and ended up trashing the place just for the hell of it."

"My laptop computer is sitting right there on my desk. There's fifty dollars in an unlocked drawer in that same desk. I put it there to pay the guy I hired to power wash the outside of the cabin next week. And the only thing I can tell was taken was a file folder I left sitting on that desk this afternoon. It contained a compilation of all the notes I had on Renee Lindsey's murder, including the ones Donnie put together before he died."

Cain grimaced. "I'm so sorry."

She pressed her lips in a tight line, struggling to maintain her composure. At the moment, she was in the mood to throw a few things around, herself. Starting with the bastard who broke into her cabin and made this disheartening mess.

"I don't suppose you have copies of those notes?" he said after giving her a moment to calm down.

"Actually, I do. At least, copies of Donnie's notes. I digitized the handwritten stuff after his death, when I was stuck home recuperating from my own injuries." She managed a grim smile, though humor was the last thing she was feeling at the moment. "Gave me something to do with my brain and my hands at a time I really, really needed a distraction."

"What about the other stuff in the stolen folder?"

She shrugged, trying to remember what else there might be. "Mostly it would have been notes I took over the past few days. I like to write things down longhand when I first make a set of notes. I got used to doing it that way when I was working as a police detective, and I never got out of the habit. I find that writing my notes in longhand helps me slow down and let my mind ferret out all the details of my observations. Typing goes too quickly."

"And you haven't had a chance to type up your longhand notes and put them on your computer?"

"Not the ones I took in the last couple of days." She tried to remember what hadn't yet been saved to her computer. "Mostly it would be the stuff about Coach Allen and our speculations about his potential relationship with Renee."

Cain frowned. "If Coach Allen is the one responsible for what happened here at your cabin—"

"Then he knows we're on to him."

Cain rubbed his jaw as he took another look around the place. "There's something strange about this mess. Don't you think?"

"As a matter of fact, yes," she agreed, following his gaze around the room. She'd understood it almost from the moment she walked into the cabin, despite the paralyzing effect of shock at the sight of so much destruction. "There wasn't any effort to make this look like a common robbery. Not even the most obvious things were taken out of here. And all the destruction is—"

"Personal," Cain finished in unison with her.

"Exactly."

"I doubt there's going to be any evidence to find," he said, looking around, "but you should probably get the break-in on the record with the cops."

The question caught her by surprise. "Cain Dennison, suggesting a call to the police?"

He grinned. "Wonders never cease."

"If you want to clear out before they come, I'll understand."

His smile faded. "You want me to leave?"

"No," she said quickly, wanting nothing of the sort. "I just figured you'd want to, considering your history with the Ridge County Sheriff's Department."

"Lotta years ago," he said with a shrug. "Maybe it's time to start acting like an innocent man instead of always looking over my shoulder."

Sara bypassed emergency services and called the station directly, telling the night-shift desk sergeant what was going on. He told her he could have deputies at her cabin in about fifteen minutes, unless she thought there was any chance the intruders might be still lurking about. In that case, he could get them there faster.

"No, I think the intruder's gone for the night." At least, she hoped so, she thought as she hung up the phone. She might be armed and well-trained, but sooner or later she'd have to sleep.

And clearly, her defenses weren't exactly shored up at this cabin. She'd locked the doors, but someone had still managed to find a way in.

"What are you thinking?" Cain asked.

"Just wondering how the intruder got in. The front door was still locked when I got here tonight." She headed into the other rooms of the small cabin, checking windows to see if they had provided the point of entry. She also checked the top of the bedroom closet to make sure her gun case was still locked. It was, and the Walther PPK was still snuggled safely in its foam mold. She locked the case, double-checked that all her extra ammunition was still in the boxes stored next to the case and headed back into the hall.

Cain stood in the middle of the hall, looking through an open door with his brow furrowed. "Is this the basement?"

"It's a root cellar."

"Is there a way down there besides this door?"

She nodded, already heading for the front door as she realized how the intruder must have gotten inside the cabin. She stopped long enough to grab a flashlight from the drawer of her desk in the front room and headed outside, Cain on her heels.

On the western side of the cabin, a door set into the ground led into the cellar. Normally, a padlock closed the door hasp to keep out intruders, but the lock lay a few feet away in the grass, snapped in two.

"Point of entry," she said flatly.

"You'll have to add a dead bolt to the door from the cellar." Cain put his hand on her arm, nudging her back toward the cabin. Sara didn't resist, as the cold wind blowing down from Sandler Ridge had a bitter edge.

She rubbed her arms to tamp down a sudden chill once they were back inside the cabin. "How does anybody know to look for me here? I haven't exactly been advertising my living arrangements."

His dark eyebrows notched upward, but he said nothing.

"Oh. Right." She pushed her hair back from her face in frustration. "Small-town gossip."

"This ain't the big city, sugar," he drawled.

But she'd felt safer in the city than she felt right now, she realized with dismay. And she was about to be spending the night here with no way to lock the door from the cellar.

Anyone could break in again, couldn't they?

"Maybe you shouldn't stay here tonight," Cain said, apparently reading her mind. "I'm sure your parents would be happy to have you stay over."

She shook her head. "You have no idea how tempting it is right now to run home to Mom and Dad. But if I do, I'll never get my life back. I can't keep running back home and hiding under my childhood bed."

Almost as soon as she'd blurted the words aloud, she wondered why on earth she was saying such an intimate, revealing thing to a man who had been little more than a stranger only a week ago.

Who was still a stranger, a few hot kisses notwithstanding.

If her confession made him uncomfortable, he didn't show it. "Then call someone to come stay here with you. At least for tonight."

Squaring her shoulders, she shook her head. "I don't need a bodyguard. I'm a trained cop, even if I'm not working at the moment." She shot him a wry look. "I'm armed and dangerous."

"You're armed?" His skeptical gaze roamed her body. "Right now?"

"Well, not at this moment. My Walther's locked in the bedroom closet. But I'm a good shot, and I have plenty of ammo."

"Have you checked to make sure your weapon's still here?"

She nodded. "When I checked for signs of forced entry."

"You know, to open that padlock, someone would have needed a bolt cutter. Was there one lying around this place before?"

She had been over every inch of the cabin while trying to assess its condition. She hadn't seen a bolt cutter or anything that could have snapped the padlock. "No."

"So someone knew you'd be gone tonight and how to get in." His eyes narrowed. "How many people in town would know those things?"

Her heart sank as she once again considered the drawbacks of life in a small town. "Really, almost anyone. My grandfather was one of those people who never met a stranger. He'd bring people into the house all the time, just to sit a spell and talk or show off his latest hunting rifle or how many cans of tomatoes he'd put up out of the garden for the winter."

"You really need to reconsider staying here alone tonight."

Before she could argue, her cell phone rang. "Hello?"

"Hey, Sara, it's Brad Ellis. I just got a call from the station—what's this I hear about somebody breaking in to your cabin?"

BEING THE DAUGHTER of a former sheriff's department investigator clearly had its perks, Cain thought as he watched three deputies scour Sara's place for clues while she talked quietly in the kitchen with Lieutenant Ellis, who'd been her father's partner before his retirement.

Cain really wasn't sure why he was sticking around at this point—she certainly didn't need him to keep her safe, at least not while her place was crawling with deputies.

But sooner or later the deputies would leave, even Ellis, and she'd be alone again.

And a lot more vulnerable than she seemed willing to admit.

He didn't doubt she was smart and tough. He didn't doubt she could use that Walther she had locked in her closet as well as she claimed. But there was no good reason for her to go it alone tonight.

Not when he could stay with her and watch her back.

Unfortunately, she had made it clear that she intended to handle the threat on her own. Her dark eyes had warned him silently against even offering his help. She apparently saw the situation as a challenge, something she had to face on her own in order to maintain her self-respect.

So he hadn't offered to stay.

But that didn't mean he wasn't going to watch her back, whether she wanted him to or not.

After ascertaining that Cain could offer no information about the break-in, the deputies had stopped paying any attention to him, making it easy for him to slip out the front door unnoticed. He stepped into the chilly night air and tucked the collar of his jacket up higher to protect his neck from the brisk wind.

He'd been worried the deputies had blocked his truck in, but they'd left him a narrow lane of escape. Not that he intended to escape far.

He backed through the gap and down the narrow drive until he reached the road. It had been a few years since he'd wandered around this part of Sandler Ridge, but if his memory hadn't failed him, there was a turnabout fifty yards up the road where he could park and watch for the deputies to leave. With the trees starting to lose their summer foliage, he'd probably even have a decent view of the cabin, a good enough view, at least, to see when the lights went out and he could safely move closer and settle in to keep vigil for the night.

His cell phone rang not long after he parked, the trill jarring in the stillness of the truck cab. He glanced at the display. Quinn, of course. Who else would be calling him at this time of night? "What's up, boss?"

"I understand there was a break-in at Mrs. Lindsey's cabin."

How the hell did he know that? "There was."

"Anything of value taken?"

"All her notes on the Renee Lindsey murder. Fortunately for her, she has backups."

"Unfortunately for us all, now someone knows everything she knows about the case."

"If it's any consolation, that isn't a whole lot." Cain grimaced in the dark, thinking about how bloody little they did know that wasn't already public knowledge, more or less. "By the way, I almost ran into Joyce Lindsey tonight. How long do you suppose it's going to be before Joyce

Lindsey figures out I'm the investigator you sent to work her daughter's murder case?"

"Not long, I'm afraid. So you'd better find out as much as you can before that happens," Quinn said reasonably. "Speaking of which, anything new going on?"

"We're still trying to get Jim Allen's DNA to test."

"*We* are?"

"Sara Lindsey and I." Cain looked toward the cabin, where the first of the three sheriff's department cruisers was backing out of the driveway.

"She's working with you now?"

"We have the same goal. And she has inside connections I couldn't dream about."

Quinn sighed softly on the other end of the line. "Are you sure you really have the same goal? It wasn't long ago that we were wondering whether she could have been responsible for her husband's death."

"She wasn't. She wants the truth as much as any of us."

"Just remember, you're my employee, not hers. Don't let her agenda change yours."

"Understood." He ended the call.

Down the road, the other two cruisers left Sara's driveway. Cain turned his gaze back to the cabin, wondering how long it would take Sara to wind down for the night.

Not that it mattered. He wasn't going anywhere.

"I'M FINE, DAD. I nailed the door from the cellar shut, so I don't have to worry about anybody else coming in that way. And I'll get a dead bolt for the door tomorrow." Tucking her cell phone under her chin, Sara finished picking up the last of the mess in the front room, tossing the ruined remains of the sofa cushions in the trash. As tired as she was, she hadn't been able to bear the thought of waking up the next day to the mess that had greeted her when she walked through the door earlier that evening.

If nothing else, she supposed, the break-in was speeding up her timetable for making a decision about what to do with her grandfather's cabin. If she was going to sell it, there wasn't much point in worrying about a new sofa, was there?

"I still think you should come stay with your mother and me," Carl said, worry darkening his voice.

"Dad, I lived alone in Birmingham for three years. Believe me, that's a hell of a lot more dangerous than spending tonight in this cabin." She wasn't sure she was speaking the truth, but she knew with certainty that running home to her mommy and daddy was a step backward, not forward.

"Do you know what the intruders were looking for?" her father asked.

So Brad Ellis hadn't let him in on that part of the investigation. She supposed she should be grateful her father's former partner had bothered to hold anything back at all.

She kept her answer purposefully vague. "They just took some papers. Nothing really valuable." Not in monetary terms, anyway.

"What kind of papers?"

So much for vagueness. "Notes and stuff."

"On Renee Lindsey's murder?"

"Yeah."

Her father was silent for so long she started to wonder if the call had cut off. But as she opened her mouth to say her father's name, he spoke in a low, tense voice. "I haven't been given permission to tell anyone this, but I'm not going to keep it from you, since you have a vested interest in the case. Brad told me they got a rush job done on the DNA in the Ariel Burke case."

Sara paced toward the front window, her heart in her throat. "The comparison to the DNA of the baby Renee was carrying?"

"Yes." Her father's voice deepened to a growl.

"And?"

"The fetuses definitely shared a father."

Chapter Thirteen

Sara had suspected the DNA would show a match. She'd even expected it. But hearing her father say the words aloud hit her like a body blow. Groping for one of the kitchen chairs, she took the weight off her suddenly wobbly knees. "Can the DNA tell you anything about the father?"

"We just know that he's Caucasian. I guess if the county could afford to do a more detailed analysis, we might be able to narrow down what part of the world his ancestors came from, but what we really need is a suspect. Without that, the DNA doesn't do us much good."

She started to turn away from the window, but

a glint of reflected light outside caught her eye. Pushing the curtains open, she peered down the hill and saw a truck parked across the road from the cabin, mostly hidden by the shadows. Only the faint glint of moonlight on the chrome of the front bumper gave its position away.

Cain Dennison's truck, she thought. Hadn't he left hours ago?

"Why don't I come by and give you a hand with the clean-up?"

"Dad, that's not necessary—"

"Is it a crime to want to see your daughter? Just humor me."

She couldn't hold back a smile. "Fine. In the morning, though. I'm going to bed." *Eventually,* she added silently, her gaze still fixed on the truck parked at the bottom of her driveway.

"Call me when you wake up in the morning," he said firmly.

"Will do. Love you, Dad. Give my love to Mom, too."

Ending the call, she peered through the window, trying to get a better look at Dennison's truck. She ended up hunting down her grandfather's ancient pair of binoculars to see if Dennison was still inside.

He was, she saw with a quick adjustment of the binocular lenses. He sat in the driver's seat, his head tipped back against the headrest and his eyes closed. For a heart-stopping second, she began to wonder if he was still alive, but then he suddenly moved, his face screwing into a frown. After a moment, his expression relaxed.

He planned to stay out there all night, she realized. Playing sentinel for her.

Torn between gratitude and exasperation, she went to her bedroom to grab a jacket. If he was going to play bodyguard for her tonight, he could damned well do it inside a warm cabin.

"YOU KNOW THE story of Crybaby Falls, don't you?" Renee's voice floated to him across the wooden bridge. He'd moved ahead, walking off his anger, while she'd lingered to pick wildflowers that grew in a riot of color near the edge of the falls.

"You mean the Cherokee woman who threw herself off the bridge because her man was killed in battle?" He turned a scoffing look her way. *"My grandmother says that's bull. No self-respecting Cherokee woman would be that stupid."*

Renee made a face at him. "You don't have a romantic bone in your body, do you?"

I could, *he thought, taking in the simple beauty of her, standing at the other end of the bridge looking at him with her head cocked and her eyes thoughtful.* I could be as romantic as you want. As romantic as you need.

"I'm pregnant," she said.

It took a second for the words to slice through the haze of his desire. And even when they registered in his foggy brain, he couldn't believe he'd heard her correctly.

"You're what?"

She walked slowly across the bridge, coming to a stop a couple of feet away from him.

The expression on her face was somewhere between sad and hopeful as she pressed her hand against her still-flat belly. "I'm pregnant. And I'm going to keep the baby."

Cold enveloped his body, starting in his limbs and rising upward to his chest, where his heart thudded a hard, slow rhythm of dismay. "Who?"

She shook her head. "I'm not telling anyone. It's for the best."

"But he owes you—"

"Maybe he does. But he's not going to give me what I need. I've finally realized it." She touched his hand where it lay on the railing of the bridge. "You're so smart, Cain. Too smart to let romantic notions lead you astray. It's why you'll never have a broken heart."

His heart felt shattered at the moment, but he supposed she was right about one thing. He'd never put his hopes in having her. Desires, yes. Dreams, perhaps. But never hope.

"What did he say when you told him?" he asked.

"I didn't. You're the only person I've told."

"Then how do you know what he'll do about it?"

"He doesn't have room in his life for my baby. Not anymore. I won't make him choose." Renee's lips curved in a faint smile. *"It would be needlessly cruel to ask him to pick which one he wants."*

A sharp knocking noise jerked Cain out of his doze. Bright light angled through the window of his truck cab, piercing his eyes and making him squint to see the dark-haired woman standing outside his window.

Renee, he thought, and then checked himself when he saw Sara Lindsey's brown eyes staring back at him through the window.

"You planning to stay here all night?" she asked through the glass.

He sat up straighter and started to roll down the window. But she was already coming around to the other side of the truck. Leaning across, he unlocked the passenger door to let her in.

She pulled herself into the seat beside him, one dark eyebrow cocked. "You were going to stay out here all night?"

"You said you didn't need anyone to watch your back." He rubbed his jaw, feeling the beginnings of a beard. "You didn't say anything about someone sticking around to watch your house."

Her lips twitched at the corners. "Sorry I startled you. When I knocked on the window, I mean."

"It's okay. I was having a dream...." He frowned, straining to remember snippets from the dream. It seemed important somehow. "A memory, really. Something from the last time I saw Renee before her death. We'd met at Crybaby Falls. We met there a lot—it was just about her favorite place on earth."

"Oh, right. The whole romantic suicidal Cherokee-princess thing."

"Yes." He rubbed the lingering sleep out of his eyes, his mind wandering back to that gloomy day at the top of Crybaby Falls. "That was the day she told me she was pregnant."

Sara turned to look at him. "Why didn't you ever tell anyone about her pregnancy?"

"She asked me not to. Not until she could tell her parents. I guess she never got the chance." He stifled a yawn. "But I think I just remembered something important. Something she said about the baby's father."

"Something you didn't remember before?"

"It's not so much that I didn't remember before. I just didn't give it the same importance as I do now. And you have to remember, back then I was trying to keep my own backside out of jail."

"So you weren't exactly volunteering information?"

"No."

"But the pregnancy was a motive for murder. If the father knew—"

"He didn't know. She didn't tell him."

"She didn't tell him?" Sara sounded surprised.

"I know we've been assuming the pregnancy was the motive for Renee's murder—"

"Ariel's, too," Sara interjected.

He looked at her. "We don't know those pregnancies are even connected."

"We do now." She told him about the call from her father. "The DNA was a sibling match to Renee's fetus."

As the full implications sank in, a shiver run through him, not unlike the chill he'd experienced that day eighteen years ago on Crybaby Bridge. "My God. I mean, we suspected it was possible, maybe even probable—"

"I had the same reaction," she confessed, tucking her thick sweater more tightly around her. The night had grown frigidly cold, Cain realized. They should be inside her warm cabin, not sitting out here in his truck.

"I don't know about you, but I'm about to turn into a block of ice. Think you could handle someone watching your back from inside your nice, warm cabin?"

At her nod, he started the truck's engine and

drove up the gravel drive, parking behind her truck. He followed her up the porch steps and waited for her to unlock the door.

Inside, the cabin was warm and much cleaner than he'd left it, he saw.

"Sorry, the sofa is a loss, but grab a chair. Are you hungry?" Sara shrugged off her sweater, revealing a figure-hugging long-sleeved T-shirt that skimmed the top of her jeans, giving Cain a peek at her bare belly and the curve of her hips as she reached into the cabinet for a skillet. "I'm not much of a cook, but even I can handle a midnight omelet."

"I could eat an omelet." He pulled up a chair and sat at the kitchen table, where he could watch her work. "How long did it take to clean up the mess?"

"A couple of hours." She put the pan on the eye to heat and retrieved a carton of eggs from the refrigerator. "Two or three?"

"Two is great." As he watched her expertly crack the eggs, he realized she might be underselling her culinary skills.

"How sure are you that Renee didn't tell the baby's father about her pregnancy?" she asked.

"Pretty sure. She died the next day." He remembered something else from that day, something he'd forgotten until the dream brought it back. "And she said something really strange that day. She said she wasn't going to ask him to choose."

"Choose what?" Sara looked at him over her shoulder. "Between her and some other girl?"

"I guess I always assumed that's what she meant. But what she actually said was that there was no point in asking him to pick which one he wanted."

She turned to face him, her eyes narrowing. "Which *one?*"

He nodded. "That's what she said. Which one."

"What do you think she meant?"

"I don't know," he admitted. "I guess maybe, thinking of what she said and how she said it— what if she wasn't the only girl her mystery man got pregnant?"

"Were there any other pregnancies at Purgatory High around that same time?"

He shook his head. "Not that I remember. But maybe it wasn't anyone at Purgatory High."

Sara frowned suddenly. "Jim Allen has a seventeen-year-old son."

"You're right," he said, suddenly feeling queasy.

"Which means Becky Allen and Renee would have been pregnant around the same time." She turned to look at him. "And maybe Renee found out about Becky's pregnancy."

"It would have changed the whole equation."

"If she thought he was in an unhappy marriage, maybe she was foolishly romantic enough to think she could win him away from Becky," Sara said in a hushed tone. "But married with a kid on the way?"

"She must have realized then that he'd already made his choice," Cain finished for her, so many of Renee's cryptic remarks finally starting to make an awful sort of sense.

Sara turned slowly back to the stove and continued preparing their omelets in silence. Cain could tell from the stiffness of her spine that what they'd just discussed had disturbed her deeply.

"I didn't want to believe it was Jim Allen," she said after a moment. "I figured after my session with your grandmother, when I didn't remember anything else, that I was maybe conflating days in my head. Maybe I was remembering a visit that didn't happen the night of the accident."

"But you were gung ho to confront him. You wanted to get his DNA."

"I think I wanted to exonerate him," she admitted, removing the skillet from the stove eye and cutting off the flame. She turned around to look at him, her expression grim. "I still want to believe there's another answer. Donnie thought so highly of the coach."

"There are other seventeen-year-old kids in Ridge County. I guess it could have been some other guy with a kid on the way. Or even someone who already had a child. Renee wouldn't have wanted to drag a man away from his family, especially if there was another kid involved."

Sara shook her head. "We have to deal in the facts, not in what I want to believe. The fact is, Renee was working in the athletic office for Jim Allen. The fact is that Jim hadn't been married long at that point—he and Becky were practically newlyweds. And I told you Donnie thought the Allens had been having marital problems back then."

"So maybe the coach thought his marriage was on the rocks and got himself all tangled up with Renee, who was only a few years younger than him. And just the kind of sweet-natured, romantic girl who could mistake sympathy for love and need for commitment."

"But then Jim learned Becky was pregnant, and everything changed." Sara grabbed a couple of plates from the cabinet over the sink and spooned the omelets onto them.

"Maybe he told Renee about Becky's pregnancy before she had a chance to tell him about hers."

"And Renee realized she couldn't ask him to choose between her child and his child with his wife."

Cain took the plates from her and set them on the table while she retrieved forks. "Renee might have loved him enough to take a chance that he'd leave Becky for her, but once a child was involved—"

Sitting in the chair across from him, Sara poked at her omelet, looking as if the last thing she wanted to do was eat it.

Cain reached across the table, covering her hand with his. "I know you don't want to think Coach Allen did something so terrible. But we have to follow this lead as far as it takes us."

She looked at him thoughtfully, her expression suddenly hard to read. "If we're right about Jim Allen being the father of Renee's baby, then he's also the father of Ariel Burke's."

"And he almost certainly killed them both." Cain looked down at the omelet, his appetite long gone. He shot her an apologetic look and pushed the plate away. "I'm not as hungry as I thought."

"Me, either." She sat back in her chair, looking shell-shocked. "But why would he kill Renee? If she had no intention of telling him about the baby, how would he have even known? Could she have changed her mind?"

Cain gave it a moment of thought. Renee had seemed so resigned to having her child without any help from the father. He'd believed her when she'd said she didn't intend to tell him about the baby.

Could something have changed her mind?

"She said she wasn't going to tell anyone who the father was," he said finally. "She meant it."

"So how did the baby's father find out?"

"I don't know."

Sara pushed to her feet as if propelled by some burst of energy her slim body could no longer contain. The grim look of resolve in her dark eyes sent a shiver of alarm rocketing through him.

"Where are you going?" he asked as she started toward the front door of the cabin.

"To get answers." As she passed the antique desk by the door, she paused long enough to open the lap drawer and pull out a gleaming Walther PPK in a pancake holster. She clipped the holster to the back waistband of her jeans and grabbed a thick wool jacket from the coat tree on the other side of the door.

"And where do you plan to get those?" he asked, catching up with her before she opened the door. He closed his hand over hers on the doorknob, pulling her to face him.

Her eyes sparked flashes of fire as she met his gaze. "From Jim Allen, of course."

Answering heat fluttered low in his belly but he pushed the sensation aside. "You can't go there in the middle of the night, wave that gun in his face and demand answers."

"How stupid do you think I am?" She tried to pull her hand away from his grasp, but he tightened his grip.

"I don't think you're stupid. I think you're

desperate for answers and you think Jim Allen can give them to you."

"What if he can?" Her question came out in a tone more vulnerable than he expected. He saw her own frustration flicker over her expression at the trembling undertone of her own voice. "I can't just keep sitting around, doing nothing. I have to know what happened."

"To Renee? Or to you and Donnie?"

"To all of us." Her voice escaped in a raspy whisper. "To me. I have to know why I drove us off that bluff."

He pulled her into his arms, curling his palm around the back of her neck. She resisted briefly, then relaxed into his embrace, her cheek warm against his shoulder.

A few moments later, her hands began to move lightly over his back, a hypnotic, seductive rhythm that charged the atmosphere around them. Not even his best intentions could stop his body's instant, obvious response to her touch.

She lifted her head, gazing up at him with

fierce intent. "You should have let me know you were outside sooner," she whispered.

His pulse thudded in his throat. "So you could send me home?"

"So I could let you in," she whispered, rising until her lips brushed his. Her lips parted, her tongue darting against his upper lip.

He opened his mouth to her kiss, slid his hand over the curve of her hip to pull her closer so she could feel what she did to him. His tongue tangled with hers, tasting coffee and the underlying sweetness of her passion.

She pushed him toward the living room, reaching the ruins of the sofa before she seemed to realize that whatever she was looking for couldn't be found there. The look of puzzlement in her eyes as she took in the ruins of the sofa was so comical he couldn't hold back a laugh.

She swung her gaze to him. "I don't have a sofa anymore."

"You have a bed."

She turned a delightful shade of pink. "It was my grandparents' bed," she said in a hushed tone. "I can't have sex with a guy in my grand-parents' bed!"

He laughed harder, frustration giving way to an almost painful level of affection for the blushing woman who stood in front of him. "It's okay. I'm not going to suggest the floor. Your grandmother probably used to mop it or something."

She gave his arm a light punch. "Funny."

He cradled her face between his hands. "I could go back outside to the truck."

"No. We'll figure out something." She looked so adorably conflicted, he almost kissed her again. But kissing her was what had gotten them into this muddle to begin with.

"Got a sleeping bag? I could lay it over what's left of that sofa and sleep there tonight."

She eyed the sofa with skepticism. "Are you sure?"

"Positive."

She gave his hand a quick squeeze. "Be right back."

He walked around the living room, trying to

cool down the fire her touch had set blazing in his gut while muffled rustling noises filtered down the hallway where she'd disappeared. By the time she returned carrying a sturdy sleeping bag folded over her arm, he felt a reasonable level of control over his libido, though the look of helpless consternation on her still-pink face threatened to set him on fire again.

"I'm sorry." She thrust the sleeping bag into his hands. "I guess I'm not as sexually liberated as I thought."

He tried not to laugh again. "If it makes you feel any better, I wouldn't exactly feel right about having sex with a woman in my grandmother's bed, either. Mostly because she'd box my ears."

"You're very understanding."

He couldn't stop himself from touching her cheek. Nor was he able to keep the hunger from his voice as he whispered, "I'm very patient."

Her dark eyes blazed back at him. "Good." She rose toward him, slanting her mouth across his with a fiery intensity that nearly undid all his good intentions.

Dragging her mouth away, she stepped back and flashed a wicked smile. "Don't be too patient."

Too much patience, he thought as he watched her disappear into the bedroom, would not be the problem.

DAYLIGHT SLANTING THROUGH the narrow space between her bedroom curtains nudged Sara awake, dragging her from a dream she couldn't exactly remember but knew she hadn't wanted to end. For a second, the sound of movement in the front of the cabin made her whole body jerk into a knot, until she remembered how her eventful night had ended.

Had she really turned down sex with Cain Dennison because she couldn't bring herself to do it in her grandparents' bed?

Bringing her knees up to her chest, she buried her hot face in her hands. Why did something as natural and normal as sex make her feel like a scared teenager all over again? She wasn't a virgin, hadn't been for over a decade. She and Donnie had shared an exciting, fulfilling sex life together; even during the more stressful period of their marriage, sex had never been an issue for them.

Maybe that was the problem. She'd had a lot of great sex, but always with just one man.

Forget falling in love again—what if she couldn't figure out how to please another man?

A knocking sound from the front of the house sent her nerves jangling. Was that the door?

Footsteps sounded in the hall, and a couple of sharp raps on the bedroom door. "Sara?"

She grabbed the jeans she'd discarded the night before and tugged them on. "Yeah?"

"Your dad's at the front door."

Cold flushed through her body. "Oh, damn! He said he'd call first." She shrugged into her bra and threw a sweater over her head on her way to the door.

Cain stepped back as she jerked open the door.

"You knew he was coming this morning and didn't think to warn me?"

"I forgot," she said, shooting him a look of apology. "But he said he'd call."

"I'd suggest making my escape out the back, but he can't miss my truck parked out there." He sounded damned near panicked, she realized.

She closed her hands over his upper arms, holding him in place. Stifling the sudden urge to laugh, she made him look at her. "It's okay. I'm well past the age of consent."

"But he's armed."

She couldn't stop a chuckle from escaping her aching throat.

"Oh, yeah, laugh it up," he muttered. "You're not the one he's going to chase down with a shotgun."

She was still chuckling a little as she opened the door to her father's repeated knock. But the grim expression on Carl Dunkirk's face drove out any thought of humor. He barely gave Cain a glance, stepping inside on a cold blast of wind and putting his hands on Sara's shoulders.

Her stomach dropped like a chunk of lead. "What's wrong? Is it Mom?"

Her father shook his head. "Your mother's fine. It's Jim Allen."

Cain stepped closer, all signs of his earlier mortification gone. "What about him?"

Carl finally let his gaze settle on Cain, a hint of curiosity flickering across his face before his expression went deadly serious again. "A student found him in his car in the high-school parking lot about an hour ago. Looks like he shot himself in the head."

"He's dead?" Sara asked, torn between surprise and dismay.

Carl looked at her, regret gleaming in his eyes. "Not yet. But the doctors don't think he's going to make it."

Chapter Fourteen

Westridge Medical Center's sleek facade brought back memories for Sara. Just not the ones she most needed to recover. As she and Cain followed her father through the front doors of the Knoxville hospital, the faintly antiseptic smell of the place hit her like a gut punch, and she stumbled over the large rug that stood in front of the sliding glass doors.

Cain's hand slipped under her elbow, keeping her from falling further off balance. She shot him a queasy smile, and his eyes widened a notch, but he didn't comment. He kept his hand curved around her elbow as they hurried to catch up with her father's long, quick stride.

The receptionist directed them to the waiting area of the emergency wing, where they found a couple of uniformed deputies milling near the coffee carafe and Lieutenant Brad Ellis sitting next to a teary-eyed Becky Allen and her three shell-shocked children. Becky was dressed in dark red scrubs, Sara noticed. Work attire? She had a faint memory that Becky had been working at a doctor's office when she married Coach Allen.

As Sara's father went to talk to Brad, Cain gave Sara's arm a light nudge and nodded toward Becky and her children. "Did you know Mrs. Allen was a nurse?"

"She used to work at a doctor's office in Barrowville," she answered quietly. "I guess she still does."

"Do you know what kind of doctor?" Something in Cain's tone made her look up at him. He was still looking at Becky, her eyes narrowed.

"I don't remember. Why?"

"I was just wondering how Jim Allen could

have learned about Renee's pregnancy. Or Ariel Burke's, for that matter."

"You think he learned from his wife?"

"We should find out who Becky works for. And if it turns out to be an ob-gyn, we need to find out if Renee and Ariel were patients."

The quickest way to get that answer, Sara supposed, was to ask Becky herself. But she was clearly distraught at the moment, in no condition to be interrogated about her employment.

Sara had never really considered the coach or his wife to be anything more than acquaintances. She certainly had no idea why she and Donnie would have gone to see the Allens the night of the accident. Coach Allen had been Donnie's friend, not hers, and she'd never gotten the feeling that the coach's wife saw his students as anything but people who took his time and attention away from his family.

Still, the woman had just taken a sharp shock to her system, and so far, there didn't seem to be people gathering around them to offer comfort. The news was too fresh, she supposed, and people couldn't exactly drop everything to come be with her.

"I should go talk to Becky," she told Cain. "I should probably go alone, though."

He nodded, giving her elbow a light squeeze, as if he realized how much she was dreading what she was about to do. And she *was* dreading it. It brought back too many raw memories of waking up in this very hospital, two weeks after her accident, and learning that those disjointed, terrifying nightmares she couldn't remember from her time in a coma were nothing compared to the truth of all she'd lost.

She walked over to the row of connected chairs where Becky and her children sat, not sure what she should say. "I'm sorry" seemed entirely inadequate. She'd never been the kind of person who could sit for hours offering sympathy and a willing ear. She was a doer. A fixer. Dealing with a problem, for her, meant seeking out concrete, physical needs and meeting them as well as she could.

"Sara." Becky spoke before she could come

up with anything to say. She reached her hand toward Sara, and Sara took it, giving it a gentle squeeze.

"How're y'all holding up?" she asked, knowing as soon as she spoke the words that it was about as lame a question as she could have thought to ask.

"As well as we can. I just—" She looked at her two youngest children, a pained expression in her reddened eyes. Lowering her voice, she added, "I just don't understand why this happened."

Sara looked at Jeff, the older boy. Like his mother, he was teary-eyed and shell-shocked, but when she suggested he take the two younger children to the gift shop to look for a get-well card for their father, he took his brother and sister in hand and did as she asked.

"Thank you," Becky said quietly. "I couldn't really talk very freely around the babies. They're never going to understand what their father has done. I don't understand it myself."

"You had no idea he was troubled enough to do something like this?"

Becky shook her head, wiping her eyes with a wadded tissue. "Not something this drastic, no."

"But you knew he was worried about something?" Sara pressed as gently as she could.

After taking a long, deep breath, Becky met Sara's gaze. "He was worried. And secretive. It started in earnest the night of the last Purgatory High get-together dinner. You remember it? You were there."

"The night the sheriff broke the news about Ariel Burke."

She looked stricken, and Sara wondered if she knew about Ariel's pregnancy. Did she suspect that Jim was the father of the baby?

Did she fear he'd been the person who'd killed her?

"Was she one of his students?" Sara asked carefully. At a school as small as Purgatory High, coaches often taught classes as well as coached teams. Coach Allen had taught history when Sara had been a student there.

"Not a student, no," Becky said in a subdued voice.

"But he knew her?"

"Star of the cheerleading squad? Oh, yeah, he knew her." The bitterness in Becky's voice was razor sharp. She looked up suddenly, as if realizing what she'd just revealed.

Sara was torn between pushing ahead for more information and letting Becky Allen deal with her grief in private. Even though she'd frequently questioned grieving family members about homicide cases during her time as a detective in Birmingham, something about Becky's raw pain and humiliation made Sara want to pull her punches.

She glanced toward her father and saw him still conversing with Brad Ellis. But Cain wasn't anywhere in sight.

Turning back to Becky, she opened her mouth to excuse herself for a moment. But before she could speak, Becky caught her arm in a surprisingly tight grip and bent her head toward Sara.

"There's something I have to tell you," she

said quietly, her fingers digging into Sara's arm so hard it was beginning to be painful. "There's something you need to know, something I should have told someone long before now. But Jim asked me not to."

Forgetting about Becky's painful grip, Sara leaned forward. "What is it? Is it something to do with Jim?"

"With Jim. And with you and Donnie." Becky's face crumpled. "Jim told me not to say anything, that getting involved would just make life harder for us, and it wasn't like there was anything we could have told anyone that would have changed anything."

"Is this about the night of the accident?" Sara asked. "About Donnie and me coming to visit you and Jim earlier that evening?"

Becky's eyes widened with surprise. "Oh, my God, you remember?"

"Not everything," Sara admitted. "I don't actually remember seeing you that night. I just remember standing outside your house. I think it was not long after sunset, and Donnie and I were arguing about something."

Becky's brow furrowed. "Arguing about what? About us?"

"You and Jim?" Sara shook her head. "No. Why would you think that?"

"No reason. I guess maybe I'm just looking for some clue to what Jim did this morning. He never really told me why we weren't supposed to talk about that night. Just said it would be messy for us to get involved. He was trying to get a raise at the school, and I was trying to get voted president of the Ridge County Women's League at the time, and he said someone might accuse me of giving you too much to drink that night."

"I don't drink," Sara said. "And certainly not when I might be driving."

"I know you didn't drink that night. I'm just saying what Jim said people would say." Becky's lips pressed into a tight line of teary frustration. "You sound like you suspect him of something else. Is it because he shot himself? You think he's feeling guilty about something?"

Sara didn't have a chance to answer. Jeff Allen had returned from the gift shop with his younger brother and sister. She got up, making room for the children in the chairs beside Becky. "I'll see if anyone has an update," she said with a final pat to Becky's shoulder.

She crossed to where her father and Brad Ellis were still conversing in low tones. They looked up with grim expressions as she joined the huddle. "Anything new?" she asked.

"He's still alive," Brad told her, sparing a quick glance toward Becky and the kids. "Apparently he's not a great shot, lucky for him. But it's still too soon to know if he's going to make it."

"How did this happen?" Sara asked. "Who found him?"

"One of the kids on his baseball team, Davy Lavelle. Poor kid's completely freaked out, as you can imagine."

"Was there a note?"

"Not that we've been able to find," Brad admitted. "We haven't gone to his house yet—we figured we'd wait until we knew more about his condition before we disturb Becky that way."

"I think you need to get his DNA," Sara said flatly.

Brad's brow furrowed. "His DNA?"

Sara's father looked at her through narrowed eyes. "You think he may have fathered Ariel Burke's baby, don't you?"

She nodded. "And Renee Lindsey's, too."

"What would make you suspect Jim Allen of all people?" Brad glanced across the room at Becky and the kids, and Sara could imagine what he was thinking. Even red-eyed and in shock, Becky Allen was still as beautiful now as when she'd been Purgatory High's homecoming queen and snagged the heart of the cutest guy on the baseball team. Maybe even more beautiful, as time had only enhanced her classic looks. Why would a man with a woman like that at home ever think of straying?

She didn't know the answer. She only knew

that in her experience as a cop, she'd learned that a good-looking wife at home was no guarantee a man wouldn't cheat.

"Did Cain Dennison put that idea in your head?" her father asked.

"I'm capable of coming up with ideas without help," she said more sharply than she intended.

Her father's eyebrows notched upward at her tone. "Fair enough."

She shot him a look of apology. "I remembered something about the night of my accident that made me question whether Jim Allen might be hiding something." She told them about her memory of arguing with Donnie outside the Allens' home. "And Becky just now confirmed that we were there that night."

"You're kidding me." Her father looked dumfounded. "We begged people to come forward with information about what the two of you were doing in town that night. Nobody did. And you're telling me Jim and Becky knew all along where you'd been?"

"Becky told me Jim convinced her not to tell.

He said it was because they didn't need to get mixed up in a police investigation, with him being a teacher at the high school and her running for Women's League president."

"That's no sort of reason." Brad shook his head.

"Did you remember why you were there?" Carl asked, his hand closing over her shoulder, warm and firm.

She shook her head. "And I didn't really get a chance to ask Becky before her kids came back from the gift shop."

"I didn't realize you and Donnie were friends with the Allens," Brad said, slanting a look toward Becky Allen.

"We weren't. That's what's strange about it." Movement in her peripheral vision caught her eye, and she spotted Cain standing near the exit. He gave a slight nod in her direction. "Excuse me a minute," she said, already moving away from her father and Brad.

"Didn't think I should just be loitering around the waiting room, annoying your father and drawing attention," Cain said quietly as she walked outside with him. Nodding toward a bench a few feet away, he led the way, and they settled there, warmed by a shaft of mild sunshine. "What did Becky have to say?"

"More than I expected," she admitted, telling him what Becky had revealed about the night of her accident. "It was so strange, hearing her talk about an event she so clearly remembered. And I can't remember any of it."

"Maybe if you could go back to their house or something…"

"On what pretext?"

"Maybe to pick up some things for Becky. Sounds like Jim has a chance of surviving, but if he does, he'll be here for a long haul. Not just because of the injury, but for psychiatric evaluation, too."

"Actually, why don't I offer to take the kids home? At least the two little ones. Being here, seeing Jeff and their mother in so much turmoil, has to be scaring them to death. I could stay with them until Becky can arrange for someone to watch them." And while she was there, she could have a look around, see if anything jogged her memory.

Cain nodded. "Good idea."

"Meanwhile, find out where Becky works," she added, lowering her voice as a couple of women dressed in scrubs passed them on their way into the hospital. "There has to be some way that Jim Allen found out about Renee's pregnancy. If Becky worked for Renee's doctor, that might be how."

"Are you sure you're okay to go to the Allens' place by yourself?"

She slanted a look at him, surprised by his cautious tone. "I was a cop for years, you know. I reckon I can take care of myself. Or are you talking about the babysitting part?"

His lips curved slightly at her final question, but the smile faded quickly. "Actually, I was thinking about the fact that you still have a big gap in your memory of the night your husband died, and part of that missing time was apparently spent in that house you're about to go looking through. What if you do remember something? Something you don't want to remember?"

Her stomach turned a queasy flip at the thought. He had a point, she knew. If there was no physical reason why she shouldn't be able to remember the missing hours from that night, as the doctors had told her, why wasn't she remembering it?

What had she experienced that her subconscious didn't want to deal with?

"Maybe you shouldn't go to Becky's house alone," Cain said quietly.

"I can't exactly make the offer to watch her kids, then ask if I can take a friend." She straightened her back and stood. "I'm fine. I'll get the kids settled and distracted from their worries, and then if I get a chance, I can look around. See if anything triggers any memories."

Cain rose as well, his fingers brushing her arm. A tingle of raw physical attraction jolted through her at his brief touch, but eclipsing even that was a sweet, bracing warmth that seemed to flow between them.

It felt like more than just sexual attraction, she realized. It felt like a real connection. Something that might have a chance of lasting, if that's what she wanted.

Was it what she wanted?

"If you need me, call," he said quietly.

"I'm not going to need you," she said, making herself pull away from his touch. They were getting too close too quickly. She wasn't ready to feel something powerful enough to change her life.

Was she?

Cain's eyes narrowed. "Is something wrong?"

She shook her head, swallowing a sudden flood of fear. She reentered the E.R. and headed toward the bench where Becky still sat with her scared-eyed children, sparing a last, quick glance at Cain, who peeled off toward her father. He met her gaze, his expression troubled, before he turned away.

Sara turned her attention to Becky. "Still no word from the doctors?"

Becky shook her head. "They said it might be a while before we know anything new."

"Why don't I take the younger kids back to your house?" Sara suggested, taking the empty seat next to Jeff. "They could probably use a break from the stress. I could get them settled down watching a movie or something and stay with them until you can arrange for someone to be with them more permanently."

Becky cocked her head, her blue eyes soft with gratitude. "You don't mind doing that?"

"I don't mind. I might need driving directions, though. I haven't been over in that area in a while."

"Of course." While Sara dug in her purse for a pen and piece of paper, Becky asked her two younger children, Gracie and Jonah, if they would like to go home for a while. "Miss Sara is an old friend of your daddy's and mine, and she can take you home and let you watch movies."

"I could pop some popcorn, too, if you like,"

Sara offered, handing the pen and paper to Becky to write down directions to the house.

The offer didn't evoke any excitement from the two younger kids, but they got up willingly enough when Sara rose to leave.

"Don't let them get into the candy at the top of the cabinet in the kitchen," Becky warned. "I'm saving that for Halloween."

"Got it." With an encouraging smile toward Becky and her older son, Sara led the two younger children outside and across the access road to where her truck was parked. She shot a quick look at Cain as she passed him on the way out, and he answered with a slight arch of his eyebrows.

Once she got the two kids strapped into seat belts on the bench seat behind her, Sara took the interstate south toward Purgatory. While she drove, she contemplated what route to take once she got to the Purgatory exit. There were quicker ways to reach the Allens' house in Quarry Heights, but she decided on Black Creek Road once she took the turnoff toward town. The mountain road was by far the most winding and treacherous, but for whatever reason, the night of the accident she and Donnie had chosen to take that road.

Maybe taking that road now would jog her memory.

The best route to the interstate highway that would take them back to Birmingham was Madison Park Boulevard, not Black Creek Road, so it wasn't likely they'd been heading out of town that night. But they hadn't called her parents or his to let them know they were in town and were planning to stay. And as far as anyone had ever been able to discover, they hadn't booked a room at any of the handful of motels in the area, and the cops had gone as far away as Knoxville and Chattanooga to check. Apparently they'd planned to stick around that night.

But to do what?

She tried to picture herself behind the wheel of Donnie's old truck, the one she'd been driving the night of the accident. She'd have been driving down this road, coming from the opposite direction. Instead of bright sunlight filtering through the trees overhead, there would have been little more than the pale glow of moonlight.

What had she seen? What had driven her off the road?

And what had any of it to do with Jim Allen?

Chapter Fifteen

Cain had turned thirty-six in June. He'd spent years in the Army, years out in the world, making his own way and being his own man.

So why the hell did he feel like a tongue-tied teenager when he thought about talking to Carl Dunkirk?

The fastest way to find out where Becky Allen worked, short of asking the woman herself, was to ask someone who knew her. And Carl Dunkirk knew everybody in Ridge County, probably better than they liked. He'd been a deputy for decades, working a job where knowing other people's business was part of the job description.

But he'd also been one of Cain's biggest detractors back when Renee Lindsey's body had first shown up at the base of Crybaby Falls. He'd hounded Cain—much to the delight of Cain's father—certain that Renee's friendship with him had been her downfall.

Hell, maybe it would have been, eventually. Cain had never understood himself why she seemed so determined to hold on to their friendship. She had been the kind of girl who could have done big things in life if she'd wanted to.

Renee hadn't needed someone like him holding her back, but whenever he'd tried to take a step away from her, she'd refused to let him go.

"You have something to say?" Carl's deep voice drew Cain's mind out of the past. He looked up to find Sara's father watching him with wary eyes. Brad Ellis had gone to talk to Becky Allen, he saw, leaving Carl standing alone near the admitting desk.

Cain took a step closer, amused by how awkward he felt approaching the older man. He felt eighteen all over again, antsy and guilty, even though he'd done nothing wrong. Well, nothing but trying to get the man's daughter into bed. And hoping he'd get a chance to try it again.

Though Sara's sudden withdrawal had caught him flatfooted. Was she having second thoughts about following through on what they'd started the night before?

Taking care to hide his thoughts, he lowered his voice. "Do you know where Becky Allen works?"

The question seemed to catch Carl by surprise. His eyebrows lifted. "Why?"

"I noticed she's wearing scrubs. Does she work at a hospital?"

"She works for Dr. Reed Clayton over in Barrowville."

"Private practice?"

Carl nodded. "Only OB-GYN in the county."

Cain released a long, slow breath. "Has she worked there long?"

"For years." Carl's gaze narrowed. "Why do you ask?"

"Was she working there eighteen years ago?"

Carl didn't answer immediately, but Cain saw the wheels turning behind his dark eyes. "Yes," he answered in a tone so grim it made Cain's gut twist in a knot.

"Was Dr. Clayton Renee's ob-gyn?"

Carl nodded slowly. "Probably Ariel Burke's, too."

"Someone should check on that." Cain rubbed his hand over his jaw, turning his gaze toward Becky Allen, who was holding her son's hand tightly as she quietly answered whatever questions Brad Ellis was asking.

"You think that's how Jim Allen found out the girls were pregnant. You think he was the father of those babies." Carl's gravelly voice drew Cain's gaze away from Becky's tearstained face.

"Yes. We need that DNA sample."

"I'll talk to Ellis."

A couple of men dressed in the dark-pants-and-white-shirt uniforms of the Ridge County EMS strode toward the door, their heads together in conversation. Brad Ellis rose from the waiting-area sofa and hurried to intercept them before they reached the exit.

When Carl crossed to join them at the door, Cain went with them. They reached the others just as Brad was asking, "Was he ever conscious at any point of the rescue?"

"Just briefly, right after we got there," the taller of the two emergency medical technicians answered, his blue-eyed gaze flickering toward Cain briefly. His eyebrows notched upward, and Cain realized the EMT had been a classmate years earlier. One of Josh Partlow's buddies on the football team, he thought. Couldn't remember the name.

"Did he say anything at all?" Carl asked. If Brad Ellis minded the older man butting in on the interrogation, he didn't show it.

"Gotta say, it was pretty weird," the shorter EMT admitted with a shake of his head. "Guy shot himself in the head. Those don't usually turn out to be talkers. I guess he lucked out and aimed poorly. Small caliber, too—anything bigger and we'd have been waiting for the under-taker."

"What did he say?" Cain asked. Both Carl and Brad Ellis shot him questioning looks, but he ignored them.

"He said, 'She's crazy. Don't let her hurt her.'"

Brad Ellis looked puzzled, but Carl's dark gaze met Cain's. "She?"

"That's it, but he said it twice," the taller of the two men said. "Then he lost consciousness and we scooped and ran."

"Thank you," Ellis said quietly, looking at Carl. After the two EMTs left, he lowered his voice. "Do you know what this is about, Carl?"

Carl looked across the room at Becky Allen, his expression grim. "I'm afraid I'm beginning to."

SARA HAD NO conscious memory of having been at the Allens' house before, but a sense of déjà vu dogged her steps up the neat stone walkway into the pretty split-level brick-and-clapboard house in the middle of Alabaster Circle. Behind the house, a sprawling backyard ended at a fence about twenty yards from a shallow bluff that overlooked Warrior Creek.

Less than a mile down that creek, Sara knew, Warrior Creek spilled its rushing waters over Crybaby Falls.

So easy for Jim Allen to walk the mile along the creek bank to the falls, she thought. Renee Lindsey had loved Crybaby Falls, Cain had told her. She was a romantic, stirred by the notion of tragic love. Had she been the one to suggest Crybaby Falls as their secret meeting place?

What about Ariel Burke? Had Jim Allen remembered his secret trysts with Renee Lindsey at the falls and coaxed young, foolish Ariel to meet him there as well?

"Can we watch *Scooby-Doo?*" Jonah asked before they'd gotten through the front door.

Sara looked at Gracie, the older of the two. At eleven, she was on the cusp of adolescence and showed every sign of being as beautiful as her mother. She was also the more solemn of the two, the weight of tragedy darkening her soft green eyes as she met Sara's questioning gaze. "It's okay," she said. "Mama lets him watch it all the time."

"*Scooby-Doo* it is," Sara said, locking the door behind them.

Gracie got the DVD from a cabinet in the living room and put the disk in the player while Jonah settled in front of the coffee table, his small fingers flicking over the chess set that took up half the glass surface. He picked up pieces and put them back, his brow furrowed as he looked down at the board.

Gracie punched a couple of buttons on the remote and the movie came on. Jonah picked up the black king from the board and clutched it in his little fist as he settled back to watch the movie.

Gracie detoured to Sara's side, her green eyes full of heartbreaking maturity. "Daddy plays the black pieces," she said quietly. "He's teaching Jonah to play." She blew out a deep sigh that broke Sara's heart into a dozen little pieces. "He was, I mean."

Sara wanted to put her arms around the little girl and hold her so tightly that nothing bad could happen to her again, but Gracie was sending off all sorts of "don't touch me" signals. Sara settled for flashing her a gentle smile. "He will again. As soon as he comes back home."

Gracie looked up at her as if she saw right through Sara's bravado. But she said nothing else, just crossed to sit by her brother on the sofa. Sara saw her sneak her hand toward the chessboard, nab the black queen and curl her own little fist around the piece.

Blinking back stinging tears, Sara retreated into the kitchen. It was a large, airy room, full of warm colors and homey smells. At one end of the room, a rectangular table filled a large breakfast nook. Sara wandered over there and sat down in one of the side chairs, trying to remember.

She and Donnie had been here, in this house, that night. Why couldn't she remember it?

She tried to picture Jim Allen sitting at the head of the table. He had always been a friendly man, a man who spoke easily, joked freely and told great stories. A charming man. A man who never met an adversary he couldn't turn into a friend.

What was that story he'd told her one time, about the pig farmer and the Bible salesman—

She sat up straighter. He'd never told her a story like that before. She'd never been close with him. So why did she remember hearing him tell that joke so clearly?

"Miss Sara?" The sound of Gracie's voice sent a jolt of raw adrenaline racing up Sara's spine.

She quelled a jerk of surprise and managed to smile at the solemn-faced little girl. "Yes?"

"My kitten is all grown up now. You want to see her?"

A flash of memory flitted through Sara's mind. A tiny white kitten with just a hint of chocolate on her nose, paws and tail. "Sure," she said, rising to take the small hand Gracie extended toward her.

Gracie led her up the short flight of stairs to the second level and into a small room with lavender walls and a small bed with a frilly white comforter dotted with tiny purple violets. On the pillow, a sleek Siamese cat blinked sleepy blue eyes at their arrival.

"She was little the last time you saw her," Gracie said, picking up the cat and curling her arms around her. "Isn't she pretty?"

The cat purred with contentment, sliding one paw up to curl around Gracie's neck. Sara smiled, remembering how much she'd always liked cats as a girl. She'd missed having pets when she and Donnie lived in Birmingham, but their jobs had made it impossible to give a pet the attention it deserved.

"She's beautiful," Sara said, hearing Donnie's voice whispering in her ear as surely as if he were standing right there in the room with them.

He *had* been, she remembered with a start. He'd been standing right there in Gracie's room beside her as the little girl—three years younger on that fateful night—had showed off her new kitten to them while her parents set the table downstairs.

"When this is over," he'd said softly, "we're going to get ourselves a cat. I promise, we're going to slow things down and get our lives back."

Tears burned her eyes as she reached out to stroke the cat's dark ears. The rumble of the cat's purr vibrated against her fingertips as she met Gracie's soft gaze. "Gracie, you remember meeting me before, don't you?"

Gracie nodded. "You and your husband. He was nice."

Sara smiled. "He was."

"Mama said he died. I'm real sorry."

Sara squelched the urge to stroke the child's soft cheek. "Thank you."

Gracie blinked hard, as if she were fighting off tears. "I'm going to go check on Jonah. He might do something naughty if I don't watch him. Mama says you have to keep an eye on him all the time or he'll get into all sorts of things he shouldn't." She set the cat back on her pillow, where it curled up and settled back down for a nap.

Sara followed her downstairs, feeling as if she were floating on a sea of ice. Chill bumps raced up and down her arms and legs as she left the little girl in the living room with her brother and returned to the kitchen.

She sat at the table, clutching the edge as the mental ice shattered into a thousand little pieces, each fragment a snippet of memory. This table. This room. The kitten, Gracie's gap-toothed grin, little Jonah's newly skinned knee—"He's as clumsy as his daddy," Becky had told them with a rueful smile—and the look of worry in Jim Allen's eyes as Donnie started asking a lot of inconvenient questions after dinner.

Questions about his relationship with Renee.

Sara hadn't been expecting the third degree any more than Jim had, and she'd tried to coax Donnie into leaving, aware that an ambush was no way to get the answers he was seeking. All he'd done was alienate Jim Allen and turn Becky into a nervous mess. She'd fluttered around, playing the consummate hostess, trying to soothe the unexpectedly roiling waters.

"Miss Sara?" Jonah Allen's quiet voice jerked her back to the present. She blinked away the memories, meeting the little boy's red-rimmed eyes.

"Yes?"

"I'm hungry."

Sara looked at her watch and realized it was nearly noon. "What would you like?"

"Chicken noodle soup?"

"I can handle that," she said with a smile, pushing to her feet. She quelled the tremble in her knees and crossed to the cabinet to see where the Allens might keep their canned soup. "What about Gracie?"

"I'm not hungry," Gracie called from the living room.

"Well, pretend like you are. What would you want?"

Gracie was quiet for a moment, then she said, "I guess chicken noodle soup for me, too."

She looked down at Jonah, who was watching her with curious eyes. "You need something else?"

"Is my daddy going to die?"

Sara felt her heart shatter. Kneeling, she put her hands on his shoulders and looked him straight in the eye. "I know he's in a very good hospital with some very good doctors." Westridge was one of the best hospitals for trauma cases in the state. If Jim Allen had any chance of surviving his self-inflicted wound, he was in the right place to make it happen. "And he's a strong guy, right? Big, tough guy."

Jonah nodded. "He's like a superhero."

"That's right. So you keep thinking about that, okay? Your daddy's going to fight as hard as a superhero to get better and get home to y'all. Right?"

Jonah nodded. "Right."

Sara watched him head back into the living room, hoping she hadn't just given him false hope. Then she turned back to the pantry and started searching for the canned soup.

Opening the door of the cabinet over the sink, she found not cans but several small bags of hard candy. They were stored in plain plastic bags, tied up with shiny foil twist ties. There were a variety of colors—red, green and some pale yellow ones that made Sara's lips purse at the mere sight. She picked up the bag of yellow candies and removed the twist top. A sharp scent rose from the bag and stung her nose.

Lemon drops, she thought, another memory bolting through the mists of her fragmented memory.

"I made them myself," Becky had said with a too-bright smile as she offered the cut-glass bowl full of sugar-crusted lemon candies, the desperate hostess trying to bring order to the chaos Donnie had created with his sharp questions for Jim.

Uncomfortable with Donnie's sudden aggressive demeanor herself, Sara had smiled an apology and taken one of the candies. But after one taste of the too-tart piece of candy, she'd discreetly slipped hers into a napkin and into the trash can nearby.

Donnie, however, had eaten his lemon drop with unnerving calm, looking like a shark toying with his hapless prey. Sara had never seen that side of her husband before, and it had been utterly unnerving.

"She helped you grade papers," Donnie had continued, refusing to be deterred by the trappings of decorum. "Renee spent a lot of time with you, didn't she? After hours when everybody else was gone." Donnie's tone had been as sharp as a hunter's arrow.

Sharp enough to cut through flesh and bone.

Jim had blanched, Sara remembered, but Becky... Becky had looked almost pleased. Her expression had been placid enough, but there had been satisfaction gleaming in her cool blue eyes, as if she were secretly enjoying her husband's discomfort.

She knew, Sara thought, her stomach knotting. Becky knew about Jim's affair with Renee. And she'd enjoyed seeing her husband squirm.

Donnie hadn't been the only predator in the room that night.

Chapter Sixteen

Not staring at Becky Allen was harder than Cain expected. But he didn't want to spook the woman, especially when all he had at the moment was speculation.

"We can't overlook the fact that Jim Allen shot himself," Brad Ellis said in a hushed tone. "Even if she told him about the pregnancies, it doesn't mean she knew he was the father or that either one of them would take that information and kill those girls."

"We don't even know if this suicide attempt is related to either murder," Carl admitted.

"Are we sure it's a suicide attempt?" Cain asked quietly.

The two older men looked at him. "You think someone else shot him?"

"I'm not sure of anything." He slanted a look toward Becky Allen. She was staring at the door to the E.R. bay, as if waiting for a doctor to come out and give her news. "How much longer before someone can confirm Ariel Burke was a patient of Dr. Clayton's?"

Ellis rubbed his chin. "The Burkes were out when I called. And Dr. Clayton's office won't tell us anything about any of their patients without a warrant."

"The girl is dead."

"Doesn't seem to make a difference to doctor-patient confidentiality."

Frustrated, Cain put his hands on his hips and felt a slight vibration under his right forefinger. He tugged his phone from his front pocket and saw that he'd missed a call from Sara. "I need to get this."

He headed outside and dialed her back, but the call went directly to voice mail. He left a message and went back into the waiting room.

He found Deputy Ellis and Carl Dunkirk talking to a man in surgical scrubs. He reached the small huddle as the green-clad doctor shook his head. "It's going to be days before we can try to bring him out of the coma. Just because the gunshot didn't kill him doesn't mean the brain injury won't finish the job. And I wouldn't get your hopes up about his being able to remember much if anything about what happened."

"Is it possible the wound wasn't self-inflicted?" Carl asked.

The doctor gave him an odd look. "I'm not an expert on forensics. I will tell you that there was stippling around the entry wound, so I'd guess the muzzle was within six inches of his head when it fired."

But that didn't mean he was the one who pulled the trigger, Cain thought, glancing across the room at the waiting area, wondering if Becky was watching them. What would she make of this powwow between cops, doctors and the Monster of Ridge County?

Jeff Allen still sat on the sofa, his lean body hunched forward in misery.

But Becky Allen was nowhere in sight.

He scanned the waiting area, looking for Becky's blond hair and maroon scrubs, but she wasn't there.

He grabbed Carl Dunkirk's arm, making the older man wheel around in surprise. Dunkirk scowled at him. "What?"

"Becky Allen's not in the waiting room."

Dunkirk's gaze followed the same route Cain's had—first to the sofa, where Jim Allen's eldest son sat in quiet misery, then around the room, returning finally to Cain. "Did you see where she went?"

"No."

Dunkirk strode across the room toward Jeff. Cain fell into step, murmuring a warning. "Don't scare the kid, Mr. Dunkirk."

Dunkirk's step faltered, and he turned to look at Cain. "Is that what I did to you?"

For a second, Cain was back in the interview room at the Ridge County Sheriff's Department, sweating and shaking as he waited for Dunkirk to stop staring at him and start asking questions. He'd already been one big nerve, aching from the loss of his friend and scared by the fury he saw on the deputy's face.

Before he found the words to answer Dunkirk's question, the older man put his hand on Cain's shoulder. "I'm sorry. We all wanted answers, and you seemed like the obvious one."

"And we could be wrong about Jim and Becky Allen, too," Cain warned softly.

"But you don't think we are, do you?"

Cain shook his head. "Just keep it cool with the kid. He's not likely to know anything about it, is he?"

Dunkirk glanced at Jeff. "No, he's not."

They continued toward the boy at a slower pace, sitting on either side of him. When Dunkirk spoke, his voice was gentle. "How're you holding up, Jeff? You need something to drink? Maybe something to eat?"

Jeff shook his head, looking miserable. "Mom

offered to grab something while she was out, but I just don't think I can eat anything."

"Where'd she go?" Cain asked.

Jeff looked up at him, his expression puzzled. "Do I know you?"

Cain shook his head. "I know your dad. From the high school."

Jeff's lips curled in a faint smile. "Everybody seems to know Dad from the high school."

"Small towns," Cain said with an answering smile. "Did your mother go home?"

"I think so. She said something about needing to get some insurance forms at home, and asked if I'd be okay to stay here alone." He lifted his quivering chin. "I'm going to have to be the man of the house until Dad comes home. Might as well start now."

Dunkirk rubbed Jeff's shoulder gently. "You're doing good, son. Your daddy's going to be real proud when he hears about it." His eyes met Cain's over the boy's head.

"We just talked to the doctor over there," Cain

said. "I get the feeling he thinks your dad's a real fighter."

"He is," Jeff said with a firmness his shaking hands belied. "He's the toughest guy I know."

"We'll make sure the doctor comes and talks to you in your mom's absence," Dunkirk said, pushing to his feet. He nodded for Cain to follow.

Cain caught up at the E.R. admitting desk. "Do you think she really went home?"

Dunkirk shrugged. "Maybe. Probably." His brow furrowed suddenly, and he started to look around the room again. "Where's Sara?"

He must have missed seeing her leave with the kids, Cain realized. He and Brad Ellis had been deep in conversation around that time. "She took the two younger Allen kids home to get them away from all this stress."

Dunkirk's frown deepened. "Is that all?"

Clearly, he knew his daughter well. "She wanted to take a look around, see if being back there would jog her memory. About the night of the accident."

"And what if it does?" Dunkirk asked, his tone grim. "What if Becky walks in right in the middle of a memory flash and figures out that Sara is remembering something that could incriminate her or Jim?"

Cain swallowed a curse and checked his phone. No new calls from Sara since the one he'd missed, not even an answer to the message he'd left. He tried her number and got voicemail again.

He met Dunkirk's gaze. The older man nodded. "Go. I'll get Ellis to send a cruiser for backup. Meanwhile, I'll see if we can rush that DNA match."

"Okay."

"Stay in touch," Dunkirk called after him.

Cain hit the door at a run, dodging foot traffic and slow-moving vehicles as he raced across the parking lot to his truck.

SARA TIGHTENED HER grip on the bag of lemon drops, a fuzzy feeling in her head, as if a thousand little bubbles were popping behind her eyes. The world seemed off-kilter, knocked a hair off its axis so that everything spun a fraction of a second too fast.

She could taste the tartness of the candy lingering in her memory, the sour burn that had made her roll it out into her palm and into a napkin before the sugar crystals finished melting on her tongue. Donnie was the one who liked tart foods; she preferred smoother, richer treats like good chocolate or salted caramels.

Had the Allens known that about Donnie? Had they given him something in the lemon drops that had made him tipsy? Is that why she'd been driving the Silverado that night?

She rubbed the sudden ache in her head, trying to remember what had happened next. He'd eaten the lemon drop as he'd grilled Jim Allen, asking about his relationship with Renee. He'd heard the rumors, he told the coach, about his yearly affairs with senior girls at the high school. "Like clockwork," Donnie had said, his words hard and precise.

Except they hadn't been precise, had they?

At first, perhaps, but as the scene in the living room had escalated, Donnie's movements had become loose-limbed and agitated, his words slurring and finally becoming little more than gibberish.

She'd been terrified, she remembered, afraid that his obsession about his sister's murder had finally driven him over the edge. That he'd finally snapped from the grief and anger, and it had struck her, as she grabbed his flailing arms and pulled him out to the truck, that she wasn't sure what to do next. Should she take him home to his parents, whose grief had driven them far too close to madness as it was? Should she try to drive him back home to Birmingham, even though his wild-eyed ranting was starting to scare her?

In the end, she remembered, she'd thought about her father. Her father would know what to do.

But they hadn't made it that far, had they?

Sara tightened her grip on the bag of candy, lifting it to the light, as if she could see through the pale opaqueness of the hard lumps of sugar to the poison at their centers. Were these the same candies?

"You can't eat that!" Gracie Allen's voice was tight with alarm. Sara turned to see the little girl standing in kitchen doorway, her eyes wide as she stared at the bag of candy in Sara's hand. "That's only for the bad people!"

Sara blinked. "For the bad people?"

"The people who want to hurt us," Gracie explained, her gaze never leaving the candies. "You have to put it up. Mama says we can never, ever touch it because it's only for bad people."

The knot in Sara's gut tightened. "Your mother made these?"

Gracie nodded. "She says sometimes there are bad people who want to hurt us, and so we have to have a magic potion to stop them."

"And where does she make the magic potion?"

"In the darkroom."

"The darkroom?" Another memory flitted through Sara's reeling mind. Jim Allen's voice, amused.

"We call it her secret dungeon laboratory," he'd told them with a smile when one of the kids had mentioned the photographic darkroom he'd built for Becky in the basement. "She says she's developing photographs for her night-school class, but we all think she's really building Frankenstein's monster in her spare time."

"Can I see the darkroom?" she asked Gracie.

The little girl's face blanched. "No, only Mommy can go to the darkroom! There's bad chemicals down there."

"Oh. Okay." Sara flashed the child what she hoped was a reassuring smile, even though her own stomach was aching so much she wasn't sure how much longer she'd be able to keep down the big cup of fast-food coffee she'd downed on the drive to Knoxville.

Bad chemicals, she thought, thinking of the crystal meth Cain had found in his grandmother's woodbin. Meth was volatile and dangerous, but easy to cook.

Had Becky put the drugs there as a warning

for Cain to stop nosing around Renee Lindsey's murder?

Sara tried to clear her mind, not wanting her darkening thoughts to scare Gracie. "You'd better go make sure Jonah's okay, don't you think? I'll put the lemon drops back where I found them."

Gracie looked relieved as she turned and went back to the den. Sara looked at the bag of candy, her eyes narrowing as she thought about what had happened to Donnie not long after he'd eaten one of the lemon drops.

To put it mildly, he'd started tripping out.

So, a hallucinogen? Something that could be cooked in a home lab?

Sara's head was starting to hurt from the effort of piecing together the sudden overflow of memory fragments into something that made sense. Why had Becky drugged Donnie and tried to drug her as well? Why not just poison them?

Was it possible that Jim Allen had no idea what his wife was up to?

Most poisons that would act fast enough to kill would show up in tests. At least, the toxins that could be easily created in a home lab. What about hallucinogens, though?

LSD was a possibility, though what she could remember of Donnie's agitation seemed a lot more violent than she'd ever seen in someone tripping on acid. DMT—dimethyltryptamine— could be cooked in a home lab if you knew what you were doing, though it was usually smoked, not ingested, because the body metabolized DMT too easily, eliminating the high.

She rubbed her aching forehead, starting to lose focus. She'd let the lab guys worry about what was in the lemon drops. Right now, she had to figure out whether or not it was even possible that Becky Allen had killed Renee Lindsey and Ariel Burke.

They'd assumed a male assailant in both of those deaths because manual strangulation wasn't an easy way to kill an adult. Sara could picture Jim Allen being able to overpower both girls without much trouble; he was a tall, muscular man. But was Becky large enough and strong enough to overpower those two girls?

Probably. Though she was as slender as she'd been back in her own cheerleading days, Becky was nearly as tall as her husband, and staying in shape had kept her fit and strong. Being a tall woman herself, Sara supposed she could hold her own with Becky Allen, but Renee Lindsey had been petite, and based on the photos of Ariel Burke that Sara had seen since her murder, she hadn't been a big girl, either.

If Becky had surprised them in some way and overpowered them quickly, then yes. She could have strangled both girls to death.

Sara crossed to the living-room doorway to check on the children. Both of them were engrossed in the movie, though Jonah was hugging a ragged-looking blanket to his chest and looking a little more worried than the *Scooby-Doo* gang's shenanigans would require.

Poor babies, she thought with a sinking heart. *If I'm right about your mother, your whole life is about to be turned upside down.*

She returned to the kitchen and took a look around, trying to remember more about the night she and Donnie had come to dinner with the Allens. She'd had no idea he was planning to confront Jim Allen. It had come as a shock to her as well as to the coach and his wife. Donnie had been keeping a lot of his investigation into his sister's death secret from her by then, putting a strain on their marriage.

Before the inquisition began, however, they'd been having a normal sort of conversation with the Allens, hadn't they? She had a vague memory of talking about what had been happening at the high school since their graduation, what teachers had left and what students had grown up to become teachers. Of course, Jim had also mentioned that Becky had been taking photography classes at the junior college up in Barrowville and how he'd built her the darkroom in the basement so she could develop her own photographs.

Sara had wanted to see the darkroom, she recalled. She was something of an amateur photographer herself, but she'd never tried developing her own film, and the idea had intrigued her.

But Becky hadn't wanted to show her the darkroom, claiming it was a mess.

Or had her reluctance to let Sara take a look around had anything to do with something that could incriminate her?

She needed to find that darkroom. Now.

Jim had said it was in the basement. So where was the door to the basement?

She didn't think she should ask the children. Based on Gracie's reaction to seeing Sara holding the lemon drops, Becky had put the fear of God into the children about her secrets. If she had some sort of drug-cooking lab downstairs in her darkroom, she would certainly make sure her kids never went down there to look around.

She wandered past the living-room entrance and into the narrow hallway. A short row of steps led up to the second level, where the bedrooms were, but there was a door in the wall to her left a few feet in front of the steps.

She tried the doorknob. It rattled in her hand, locked.

That was promising.

She reached into the pocket of her jeans and pulled out her key chain. From the leather tool pouch she kept on the chain, she withdrew a simple lock pick she'd bought years ago when she first joined the police force. The ability to pick a lock was a rudimentary skill for police officers, and while the doorknob lock might be effective in keeping the Allen children from going down to the basement, it proved no problem for Sara. The door lock disengaged, and she eased the door open as quietly as she could.

The basement was inky dark, and if there was a light switch on either side of the stairway, Sara didn't find it as she crept her way into the dark basement below.

At the bottom, she fumbled with her key ring until she found the small pen light attached. She snapped the light on, and the weak beam illuminated a narrow path in front of her. She swept the light around until she spotted a red bulb with a chain attached. Crossing to the light, she tugged the chain and red light spread in a circle around the center of the basement.

The setup was, at first glance, like almost every darkroom Sara had ever seen. A long table filled the center of the room, stocked with bottles of developer, pickling vinegar that Sara supposed acted as a stop bath, and fixer. Four flat plastic trays lay lined up in a row on the table, currently dry, with tongs lying next to them, and near the end of the table was a stack of black-and-white photographic paper.

But it was the large cabinet behind the table that drew Sara's attention, due to the shiny silver padlock that held its doors shut. What on earth would Becky be hiding in that cabinet that would require a padlock?

She needed to talk to Cain and let him know what she'd stumbled on. If she was making too much out of her suspicions, he'd talk her down. But if she was right…

Pulling her cell phone from her pocket, she turned it on and found, to her dismay, that her battery was critically low. She should have charged it in the car on her way to the hospital, she thought with a grimace, pocketing it as she turned to head back up the stairs to the Allens' landline.

But before she reached the bottom of the stairs, the door opened, daylight pouring into the basement in a blinding flash. A tall, slim silhouette stood at the top of the stairs, the unmistakable shape of a gun clutched firmly in her right hand.

Sara's heart skittered into high gear.

"I really, really wish you hadn't done this," Becky Allen said.

Chapter Seventeen

Sara still wasn't answering her phone. Cain didn't know whether or not he should worry—for all he knew, she was one of those people who put her phone on vibrate and never felt it when it buzzed.

There was a lot he didn't know about her, if he was honest with himself. But he wanted to know everything.

Like what she did to relax. What kind of music she liked. What foods were her favorites. What she was really thinking when she turned those dark eyes on him and seemed to stare right into his soul.

He knew she was a smart woman. He knew

she was tough and capable. But she didn't know that Becky Allen was on her way home. And she didn't know, as Cain did, that it was possible Jim Allen hadn't been the one holding the gun that had come perilously close to killing him.

The drive from Knoxville to Purgatory took a little over thirty minutes, driving as fast as he dared. At most, Becky Allen had a ten-to-fifteen-minute head start on him.

Would it be enough to put Sara's life in danger?

In desperation, he tried her cell phone one more time. Once again, the call went straight to voice mail. The fast shunt to voice mail suggested she was either on the phone or had shut off the phone altogether.

Pulling to a stop at the intersection where Sequoyah Highway crossed Old Quarry Road, Cain called The Gates, bypassing Quinn's direct number in favor of the agents' office. Ava Trent answered on the second ring. "The Gates."

"Ava, it's Cain Dennison. I need an address."

SARA TOOK A slow step backward as Becky Allen descended the stairs, the small black pistol gripped in her right hand leveled at Sara's head. "What on earth are you doing?"

Becky reached the ground level. "You're remembering, aren't you?"

"Remembering?" Sara played dumb.

"I'm not stupid." She nodded at the bag of lemon drops Sara still held. "You remembered those, didn't you?"

Sara gave up any pretense. Becky clearly wouldn't buy the ignorant act. Besides, she wanted answers, even if they were the last answers she ever got. "Donnie ate one of these lemon drops. And then he started acting strangely."

Becky almost smiled. "I wasn't sure they'd work. That's why I paid one of the addicts I know to bleed your brakes while we were at dinner. Just in case."

Sara's gut tightened painfully. "You bled the brakes?"

"Enough to make them soft. You know these mountain roads. One wrong move…"

My God, Sara thought, sickened. "Why? Because Donnie suspected that Jim had killed Renee?"

"Because he knew that I was the only way that Jim could have known she was pregnant."

"You found out from Dr. Clayton. You told Jim."

"I didn't tell Jim." Becky's whisper of a smile hit Sara like a punch in the gut. "He was as surprised as everyone else when he learned about the baby."

"He wasn't the one who killed her, was he?"

Becky laughed. "He doesn't have the backbone for it. He would have wanted to do right by the girl. Claim the kid as his own. Humiliate me in front of the whole town."

"You couldn't let that happen."

Becky's chin rose like a dagger. "No, I couldn't."

"And Ariel Burke?"

Becky's lip curled in disgust. "He never learned. Not from Renee, not from the others—"

"The others?"

"You think he never messed around with any other homecoming queens between Renee and Ariel?" Her expression darkened. "Every girl in Ridge County goes to Dr. Clayton. Only gynecologist in the county—you know how that works. Do you know how many times one of those cute little things came through the doors, looking for birth control or a pregnancy test, and every damned time I had to wonder, was Jim doing her, too?"

"Why didn't you just leave him?"

Becky looked at her as if she'd lost her mind. "You know this town. You know how fast the rumors would have flown. It would have turned into one big joke—the jock stud hero who still has what it takes get into the pants of cute little coeds versus the aging shrew of a wife who can't even keep him faithful for more than a month at a time."

"What did you give us?" Sara shook the bag of candy.

A flicker of pride gleamed in Becky's eyes, sending a shudder rippling down Sara's spine. "I just gave you lemon drops."

"Donnie started tripping almost as soon as we got out to the truck." The fragmented images that her brain had been piecing together for the past few hours had started to form a coherent memory of the night of the accident. "He hit me in the mouth, hard enough to stun me as we reached the hairpin curve. Donnie never raised a hand to me in his life." She gave the bag of lemon drops an angry shake. "What did you dose him with?"

"DMT," Becky answered finally, her tone almost bored. "Ayahuasca, to be specific. Mixed into lemon sugar syrup and allowed to harden. It's a big favorite with hard-core users."

"Not as volatile to cook as meth," Sara murmured, her gaze wandering around the basement, taking in the boxes stored on shelves at the back of the basement. Not hard to turn a darkroom into a drug lab, she knew, with the right equipment and ingredients.

Becky smiled. "I have kids. You think I'm going to cook meth?"

"You did, though. Didn't you? Enough to try to blackmail Cain Dennison into backing off his investigation."

"You can't prove that."

"It doesn't matter." Sara gave a wave toward the lab equipment. "What else do you deal in? Magic mushrooms, maybe? GHB?"

"I dabble in this and that. Girl's got to make a decent living, and God knows Jim's never going to make anything coaching high-school baseball." She laughed without a hint of humor. "He promised he was going to make it in the majors. If I just hung in there with him, he said, we'd be set for life. Yeah, that really worked out."

"Jim never asked where the extra money was coming from?"

"Jim doesn't want to know."

"Is this why he shot himself?" Sara waved her hand toward the boxes in the back of the basement. "Or did he find out you were the one who killed Renee and Ariel?"

"He was careful, after Renee." Becky shook her head. "It put a scare into him, finding out she was pregnant after her death. He'd assumed she was on contraceptives. Idiot."

"What happened with Ariel?" Sara asked, stalling for time. Right now, Becky held all the leverage in the palm of her right hand. Sara had left her own weapon in the lockbox in the bed of her truck, safely away from the Allen children.

"She told him she was on birth-control pills. No condom required."

"She lied?"

"She had a prescription. I checked. But she wanted more than a few tumbles in the back of his truck out on some dirt road in the middle of nowhere. She thought a baby would make him leave me for her." Becky flicked the pistol toward Sara, motioning for her to move deeper into the basement.

Sara stayed put. "Would it have? Made him leave you, I mean."

"Doesn't matter, does it?"

"Were you the one who broke into my cabin last night?"

Becky just looked at her.

"You heard I was helping out Brad Ellis with the investigation, right? You must have wondered if I had remembered anything about that night. So you broke in and took my notes."

"I broke in to scare you," Becky said bluntly. "Make you think you were in danger. Make you go away again. But you just dug in your heels, didn't you?"

"I'm not a foolish little teenager in love," Sara answered. "I don't scare easily."

"That's too bad for you." Becky gestured more emphatically with the barrel of her gun. "Go to the back of the basement. There's a drop cloth back there. I want you to spread it out and stand in the middle of it."

Sara's heart skipped a beat. "Easier to clean up the mess?"

Becky just looked at her without answering.

"The kids will hear the gunshots."

"I told them I'll be doing some hammering down here. Making a nice surprise for their daddy when he wakes up." Becky shook her head. "He's not going to wake up, but they don't have to know that. Not for a while."

"I'm supposed to just go along with what you ask? Make it easier for you to kill me and cover it up?" Lifting her chin with raw determination, Sara shook her head, trying not to think of everything she'd be leaving behind. There'd been a time, not so long ago, when the thought of following Donnie into the next world wouldn't have seemed like such a bad outcome.

But that's not the way she felt now. She had her parents. Friends like Kelly and Josh. Good old Brad Ellis and even Joyce and Gary Lindsey, who could finally have a little closure in the deaths of both their children, if she managed to get out of here alive to tell them what happened.

And there was Cain. Tough-shelled, soft-hearted Cain, who made her feel all the prickly, painful, wonderful sensations that came with rediscovering her life. She wanted to see if there was really such a thing as a second chance at happily ever after. She wanted to prove to Cain that he was worthy of finding his own happy ending, too.

She wanted it almost more than she wanted her next breath.

But she couldn't have any of those things if she was bleeding to death on the floor of Becky Allen's basement. She had to find a way to turn the tables and get the upper hand.

But hell if she knew how to get past a loaded .38.

THE ALLENS LIVED on a cul-de-sac surrounded by dense woods and butting up to Warrior Creek. The proximity to Crybaby Falls didn't escape Cain as he parked behind Sara's truck on the street.

There was a compact green Honda sedan parked in the driveway. Cain walked up the drive and touched his hand to the Honda's hood. Still hot. She hadn't beat him here by much.

He headed up the flagstone walkway to the

neat little house with the perfectly manicured lawn and six neatly trimmed azalea bushes flanking the brick and concrete stoop.

The Allens cared about appearances. Enough to kill to maintain them?

He started to knock on the door but hesitated, considering his options. The door was likely to be locked, though he could get past that obstacle if necessary. But could he get inside without alerting Becky Allen that he was there?

His cell phone rang, sending an electric jolt down his spine. He silenced it quickly by answering. "Dennison."

"It's Carl Dunkirk. I'm headed your way."

He wondered how Dunkirk got his cell-phone number, then realized the man used to be a cop. He had resources nearly as good as Cain's. "Has something happened?"

"Brad Ellis finally got hold of Ariel Burke's former boyfriend. Turns out the last time he saw Ariel was the morning before she was killed. And guess who she was talking to?"

"Jim Allen?"

"Becky Allen." Dunkirk's voice darkened. "I'm about ten minutes out. You'd better wait for me."

A muted cracking sound came from somewhere inside the house, setting Cain's nerves rattling. "No time," he growled, slamming the phone shut and trying the doorknob.

To his surprise, it wasn't locked.

THE SHOT CAME without warning, slamming into the wooden shelf behind Sara's head, sending splinters of wood flying into her hair and face. One sharp sliver slashed her cheek, but she barely felt it, her whole body a knot of jangling nerves.

"Get the drop cloth," Becky ordered. "Now."

Hell, no, Sara thought, lifting her chin. She couldn't see a way out of this basement alive, but she'd be damned if she made it easier for Becky to kill another woman and get away with it unscathed. "You might as well shoot me now and get it over with. I'm not going to cooperate with you."

"No fear of death? Not even a little?" Becky took a couple of steps closer, cocking her head as if examining Sara the way she might look at a bug under a microscope. "Losing Donnie do that big a number on you? Maybe you're looking forward to joining him up yonder, huh?"

"I don't want to die," Sara said with as much calm as she could muster. "But I told you, if I'm going to die today, I'm not going to do a damned thing to make it easier on you."

"I can always go upstairs and get the kids. Let them come down here and get the drop cloth for me. I'll tell them it's a game we're playing. All they have to do is get the drop cloth and go stand there in the middle of it, and they'll do it without question. They trust me. I'm their mother."

Bile rose in an unexpected rush up Sara's throat as Becky's meaning filtered through the rush of adrenaline still flooding her system. "My God, Becky. They're your children."

"They're Jim's children. And he's the biggest mistake I've ever made." Becky's lips curled with disgust. "I remember, I was so happy when I found out I was pregnant with Jeff. I thought it would solve all those little problems we'd been having after Jim washed out of pro ball. Then I overhead that stupid little girl telling that Dennison boy about the baby. And I knew. I'd seen Jim with her, you see. And he'd tell me he was just listening to her troubles, that I was being paranoid, but I knew. I could smell her on him sometimes, you know. Basil and lemon. In his hair, on his shirt. On his skin."

"That's not Jeff's fault. Not Gracie's fault or Jonah's—"

"They're constant, sickening reminders of who I shackled myself to. I thought he was a good choice. He was going places." Becky laughed again, the sound harsh with regret. "The only place he was going was right back here to Purgatory, where he could screw pretty little high-school girls and pretend he was still the hottest stud on campus."

A faint noise, coming from somewhere upstairs, seeped past the sound of Becky's voice, sending a dart of alarm skittering down Sara's spine. Had one of the kids gotten curious and decided to come looking for their mother?

Please stay upstairs, babies, she thought with rising desperation, trying not to let her attention wander away from Becky's face. *Whatever happens, stay upstairs.*

Becky's finger slid to the trigger, giving Sara just enough time to duck when another bullet smacked into the shelf behind her.

"Get the drop cloth. Now. Or I'll call the kids down here. I swear to you, I will."

Sara stared back at her, trying to assess Becky's intentions. Was she bluffing? Or was she really willing to kill her own children? Was this her way of tying up all the loose ends of her out-of-control life? First take out Jim, then her children? Freeing herself to go out and start a new life under a new name somewhere far, far away from here?

She wasn't sure. But she couldn't take the chance. If she cooperated, there was a chance Becky wouldn't harm her children.

Sara turned and walked slowly toward the shelves at the back of the basement. "Where's the drop cloth?"

"In that box with the blue lid." Becky sounded impatient.

Sara opened the box and pulled out a neatly folded plastic sheet.

"Bring it out here to the middle of the floor and unfold it."

Sara did as Becky asked, her heart pounding with growing terror. She didn't want to die. The will to live coursed through her like electricity, lighting up her nerve endings and flowing into her veins like pure adrenaline.

But she was out of options.

A flash of movement behind Becky caught her eye. The door to the basement was opening. Had curious little Gracie decided to check up on her mother?

Sara looked desperately at Becky, trying to gauge her chances at overpowering her without getting herself or one of the children killed.

Not great.

Behind Becky, the door creaked. Becky's attention snapped away from Sara for a split second, giving her the tiniest of openings.

She took it, throwing herself at Becky and tackling her to the floor just as Becky pulled the trigger.

A THIRD BARK of gunfire greeted Cain before he could get the basement door open, sending a jolt of pure terror rocketing through his body. He ducked on instinct but picked up speed, barreling down the stairs.

He hit the landing, stopping just long enough to take in the sight of Sara wrestling with Becky Allen on the basement floor. Nearby, a plastic drop cloth covered the floor, the edges nearest the women rumpled from their struggle.

Cain moved forward quickly, stepping on Becky Allen's gun hand. She cried out, a roar of pain and frustration.

With the threat of gunfire neutralized, Sara went into full-on cop mode, jerking the pistol from Becky's trapped hand and sending it sliding across the floor well out of reach.

"Help me roll her over," Sara said bluntly, looking up at Cain with a mixture of relief and some darker, richer emotion he couldn't quite discern. He did as she ordered, using blunt force to hold the struggling, cursing woman down while Sara crossed to a nearby shelf and grabbed a roll of heavy-duty duct tape.

While he straddled Becky's thighs to keep her immobile, Sara quickly secured Becky's hands behind her back. She taped up her ankles as well, pulling her feet up to hog-tie her in place.

The sound of footsteps wandering around above drew Sara's sharp glance toward the basement door. "Keep her here. I have to stop the kids from coming downstairs."

Cain watched her hurry up the stairs, his chest filling with a heady blend of admiration and affection. Sara might consider herself tough as nails, and in a lot of ways she was, but she was softhearted enough to try to protect those poor kids a little longer from the harshness life was about to throw their way. She was an amazing woman, and he hoped like hell he could find a way to convince her to take a chance on a man like him.

He turned his attention to Becky, who was growling profanities at him as she struggled to free herself from his iron grasp. If he'd had any doubts that Becky Allen was directly involved with Renee Lindsey's death, they were gone. He'd put together the clues—the gunshots, the drop cloth on the floor—and what little he'd made out of the muted conversation he'd heard coming through the basement door to get a pretty clear picture of what was going on.

Strangling Sara Lindsey to death wouldn't have worked the way it had with Renee and Ariel. Becky hadn't had the luxury of surprise, and Sara was as tall and strong as she was, unlike the two teenage girls she'd caught unaware. That's why she'd gone with the pistol.

"You were going to kill her on the drop cloth. Minimize the mess. But why kill her at all?" he asked.

Becky's answer was a profane indictment of his parentage.

"Hey, I've called my old man worse," he said with a grim smile. "Just one more question. Did you shoot your husband, too?"

Becky fell silent beneath him.

He'd take that as a yes, he thought, his mouth curling into a grimace, his gaze rising to the open door at the top of the stairs. He could hear Sara's soft voice filtering down from somewhere above, mingling with the querulous replies of the Allen children.

He closed his eyes, aching for those kids. Their lives would never be the same. He just prayed they had someone in their lives the way he'd had his grandmother. They were going to need it.

"JIM'S PARENTS ARE taking custody of the kids," Sara's father told her a couple of hours later when she emerged from her interview with Brad Ellis to find him pacing in the hallway outside.

He wrapped her up in a fierce hug, dropping a kiss on the top of her head.

"Anything new on Jim's condition?" she asked, curling her arms tightly around his waist and rubbing her cheek against his shirt, wrapping herself in the familiar, comforting smell of him. She might be over thirty now, but there was still nothing in the world quite like a father's love to make the big, bad world seem a little less scary.

"They're cautiously optimistic he's going to make it. The jury's still out on how much brain damage he might have sustained." Carl released her from the hug but kept his arm draped over her shoulders. "You free to go?"

"Almost. Brad's got to type up my statement and let me sign it." She hoped Brad was a speed-typist. She was feeling pretty shaky now that the adrenaline flood that had kept her moving had finally started to ebb. "Have you seen Cain?"

"Not since I got here."

Brad Ellis emerged from the interview room, clapping Carl on the shoulder and giving Sara's arm a light pat. "I'll get this statement typed up and back to you in no time."

"Do you know if Cain Dennison is still being interviewed?" she asked as Brad turned to go.

"He was released about fifteen minutes ago. He didn't have as much ground to cover as you did, I guess." Brad headed toward his office down the hall from the interview room.

Sara frowned. She needed to talk to Cain, but she supposed it was silly to think he'd stick around the cop shop to wait for her. She knew his aversion to police stations.

And she'd made it pretty clear to him, earlier in the hospital, that she wasn't ready to pursue the connection that had been growing between them.

How was he supposed to know that she'd changed her mind?

Her father nudged her toward a nearby bench. "I called your mother to let her know what was going on," he warned her as they sat to wait for Brad. "She's not very happy with either of us."

Sara sighed, dropping her head against her father's shoulder. "I guess this wouldn't be a good time to tell her I'm planning to stick around Purgatory and apply for a job with the sheriff's department."

"I think she's been expecting that ever since you got sucked into this murder investigation," her father said, his voice threaded with pride. "I know I was. You're a cop at heart. You always have been. I knew that the first time I caught you sneaking peeks at my case files."

Brad Ellis returned a few minutes later with a pen and a printed statement. He drew an X where he wanted her to sign, though she knew the protocol as well as he did. She scratched her signature in the appropriate place and handed the pen back to him.

"You'll be hanging around Purgatory a little longer, won't you?" Brad asked, giving her a knowing look. "In case we have more questions?"

"Yeah, I'll be around," she said with a smile.

She and her father walked down the long corridor toward the front exit, where she'd parked her truck in visitor's parking. To her surprise, Cain Dennison was waiting for her there, his long arms draped over the top of her tailgate. He nodded to her father, but his gaze locked with hers, blazing with intent. She felt an answering tug low in her belly.

"Thanks for coming, Dad," she said, tearing her gaze away from Cain long enough to give her father a fierce hug. "I'll drop by the house later so Mom can reassure herself I'm okay."

Her father gave her cheek a quick stroke, nodded back to Cain and headed toward his own truck, leaving her alone with Cain.

"Let's get out of here," Cain said.

Epilogue

The roar of Crybaby Falls grew in strength as Sara and Cain wound through the overgrown trail toward the creek. He leaned a little closer. "You hungry? Maybe we can grab something to eat a little later."

She darted a look at him, a smile curving her lips. "Together? In public?"

He smiled back, not mistaking the teasing tone in her voice. "I like to live dangerously."

"Don't take this wrong, but I'd much rather get takeout. I can't think of anything I want to do more than put my feet up and not move until Monday."

"Just 'til Monday?"

"I'm planning to apply for a job at the Ridge County Sheriff's Department." She stole a glance at him, as if wondering how he'd take the news. He'd been vocal enough about his troubled relationship with law enforcement, so he could hardly blame her for her apprehension.

His attitude toward the police had evolved over the past few weeks, he supposed. Especially if Sara was the one wearing a badge. "You'll be an asset to the department."

She shot him a grin, looking ridiculously, endearingly pleased.

Ahead, the trees began to thin out as they neared the top of the falls. He took her hand and gave it a tug. "Let's do this, Deputy."

"Do what?" She quirked her eyebrows, looking intrigued. He just smiled and motioned with his head for her to come along with him, leading her across the bridge over Crybaby Falls.

They picked their way down the slightly treacherous incline that flanked the falls. He could tell by her look of curiosity that she'd never ventured to this part of the falls. Few people did—the path was steep and scary-looking, and only daredevils and fools ever took the chance.

He'd been one of those people, both daredevil and fool. Mostly, he'd been a kid who'd felt he had nothing to lose, and the challenge had seemed impossible to resist.

He'd learned, however, that the descent was less treacherous than it looked, and worth the slight risk once he'd discovered the treasure that lay at the end of the journey.

"Oh," Sara murmured, her voice soft with surprise.

Ahead of them, the path curved toward the falls, where a set of natural stone steps led toward a hidden cavern behind the flow of water.

"Did someone make these?" she asked as they started down the steps.

"Either the Cherokees or God. Take your pick." The steps ended where the floor of the cavern leveled off to a stone shelf sheltered by the roaring curtain of water that hid them from the world outside.

"I had no idea this place existed," Sara breathed, her smile widening as she took in the full splendor of this inside view of the falls.

"Not many people do." Cain led her to an outcropping along the back wall of the cavern that formed a makeshift bench. He settled her onto the outcropping and took a seat beside her. "My grandmother showed me this place, back when I was a kid. I think it was her way of teaching me that I couldn't let fear and anger stop me from finding the beauty in this world. I think maybe more people knew about this place back then. But after Renee's death…"

"Not many people come to the falls anymore."

"Nobody but me. And teenagers looking for a thrill." Smiling, he reached down and pulled her feet into his lap. Removing her shoes, he began rubbing her feet. A look of pleasure suffused her face, and he felt an answering response building low in his belly.

"You're turning out to be rather handy to have around," she breathed, gasping as he stroked the velvety skin just below her ankle.

"I'm counting on that," he admitted. "I plan to be indispensable." He stroked his way up to her calf, making her suck in another quick breath. "Irresistible."

Her back arched a little at his light touch, stoking the fire in his blood. "You're devious. I think I like it."

He trapped her gaze with his, not hiding the desire that burned in his belly. "You have no idea the things I have up my sleeves."

She swung her legs off his lap and scooted up next to him, tucking herself firmly against his side. He slid his arm around her shoulders, pulling her close, loving the feel of her body pressed so intimately to his.

She flattened her hand over the center of his chest, then let it skim lightly, temptingly down until it rested just above the waistband of his jeans. "I have a few tricks of my own. Want to see one?"

More than he could say. But there was no hurry. Neither of them was going anywhere else for the foreseeable future. "Maybe later," he answered, brushing his lips against his ears. "Definitely later," he amended quickly, making her laugh.

With a little sigh that wavered somewhere between frustration and contentment, she settled her head into the curve of his neck and relaxed. "I'm holding you to that."

"I'm counting on it." He dropped a kiss on her temple. "I know you're scared of all this—"

"I'm not," she said quickly, looking up at him, her expression so earnest it made his heart hurt a little. "I mean, I was. But I'm not now. When I was down in the basement with Becky, and I had a million other things to think about, one of my worst fears what that I'd die before I got to tell you that I wasn't afraid anymore. I have… expectations of you."

He couldn't hold back a smile. "Good. I have expectations of you, too."

She grinned at him, snuggling closer. "Good. I like having goals."

He tucked her head beneath his chin and turned his gaze toward the rushing curtain of water, finding both solace and hope in the relentless pulse of Crybaby Falls as it carved its determined path through the unforgiving rock.

"So do I," he whispered into her hair.

So do I.

* * * * *

MILLS & BOON®

Why shop at millsandboon.co.uk?

Each year, thousands of romance readers find their perfect read at millsandboon.co.uk. That's because we're passionate about bringing you the very best romantic fiction. Here are some of the advantages of shopping at www.millsandboon.co.uk:

* **Get new books first**—you'll be able to buy your favourite books one month before they hit the shops

* **Get exclusive discounts**—you'll also be able to buy our specially created monthly collections, with up to 50% off the RRP

* **Find your favourite authors**—latest news, interviews and new releases for all your favourite authors and series on our website, plus ideas for what to try next

* **Join in**—once you've bought your favourite books, don't forget to register with us to rate, review and join in the discussions

Visit **www.millsandboon.co.uk**
for all this and more today!